JOSEFINA

Sunlight and Shadows

by Valerie Tripp

★ American Girl®

From the lookout tower, Josefina can spot visitors coming from far away!

In the middle of the house is an open courtyard with a small garden and two clay ovens.

The house has rooms for sleeping, cooking, eating, weaving, praying, and storage.

Papá
Josefina's father, who
guides his family and his
rancho with quiet strength

Ana
Josefina's oldest sister,
who is married and
has two little boys

Francisca
Josefina's fifteen-year-old
sister, who is headstrong
and impatient

Clara
Josefina's practical,
sensible sister, who is
twelve years old

Tía Dolores
Josefina's aunt, who lived
far away in Mexico City

Tía Magdalena
Josefina's godmother,
a respected healer

Abuelita
Josefina's grandmother,
who values tradition

Abuelito
Josefina's grandfather,
a trader and storyteller

Josefina and her family speak Spanish, so you'll see some Spanish words in this book. You'll find the meanings and pronunciations of these words in the glossary on page 112. Remember that in Spanish, "j" is pronounced like "h." That means Josefina's name is pronounced "ho-seh-FEE-nah."

TABLE of CONTENTS

1 Primroses.............................. 1

2 Abuelito's Surprise 12

3 A Gift for Tía Dolores................... 27

4 Josefina's Idea......................... 37

5 Light and Shadow...................... 47

6 Turning Blankets into Sheep........... 57

7 Rabbit Brush........................... 64

8 The First Love 69

9 Christmas Is Coming 82

10 Where Is Niña? 92

11 The Silver Thimble..................... 97

12 La Noche Buena 102

Glossary of Spanish Words 112

Inside Josefina's World...................... 114

Primroses

osefina Montoya hummed as she stood in the sunshine waiting for her sisters. It was a bright, breezy morning in late summer and the girls were going to the stream to wash clothes. Josefina's basket was full of laundry, but she didn't mind. She enjoyed going to the stream on a day like this. The sky was a deep, strong blue. Josefina wished she could touch it. She was sure it would feel smooth and cool.

Josefina liked to stand in front of her house, where the life of the *rancho* was going on all around her. She could smell the sharp scent of smoke from the kitchen fire. She could see cows and sheep grazing in the pastures. Tall grass rolled all the way to the dark green trees on the foothills of the mountains, and the mountains zigzagged up to the sky. She could hear all the sounds of the rancho: chickens clucking, donkeys braying, birds chirping, workers hammering, and children laughing. The sounds seemed like music to Josefina. The wind joined in the music when it rustled the leaves on the cottonwood trees. And always, under it all, was the murmur of the stream.

Josefina shaded her eyes. Even from this far away, she could see Papá. He sat very straight and tall on his horse. He was talking to the workers in the cornfield. The rancho had belonged to Papá's family for more than one hundred years. All those years, Papá's family had cared for the animals and the land. It was not an easy life. Everyone had to work hard. Some years there was plenty of rain so that the crops grew and the animals were healthy. Some years there was not enough rain. Then the soil was dry and the animals went thirsty. But through good times and bad the rancho went on. It provided everything Josefina and her family needed to live: food, clothing, and shelter. Josefina loved the rancho. It had been her home all the nine years of her life. She believed it was the most beautiful place in all of New Mexico and all of the world.

Josefina was dancing a little dance of impatience to go with the song she was humming when her oldest sister, Ana, joined her.

"Josefina," Ana said. "You remind me of a bird, singing and hopping from one foot to the other like that."

"If I were a bird," said Josefina with a grin, "I could have flown to the stream and back twenty times by now. I've been waiting and waiting! Where are Francisca and Clara?"

"They're coming," Ana sighed. "They couldn't agree on whose turn it was to carry the washing tub."

Josefina and Ana looked at each other and shook their heads. They were the youngest and eldest of the four sisters, and they got along beautifully. But Francisca and Clara, the middle sisters, often disagreed, always over some silly little thing. They reminded Josefina of goats ramming into each other head-to-head for no particular reason.

When the girls appeared at last, it was easy to see who had won the argument. Francisca, looking pleased with herself, carried only a basket of laundry balanced on her head. Clara, looking cross, carried the large copper washing tub.

Josefina put her basket of laundry into the empty copper tub. "I'll take one handle of the tub, Clara," she said. "We'll carry it between us."

Clara said, *"Gracias."* But she sounded more grumpy than grateful.

Josefina knew a way to cheer her up. "Let's race to the stream!" she said.

"Oh, no . . ." Francisca began to say. She didn't like to do anything that might muss her clothes or her hair. But Josefina and Clara had already taken off running, so Ana and Francisca had to run, too.

The sisters flew down the dirt path that sloped past the fruit trees, past the fields, and to the stream. Josefina and Clara reached the stream first, plunked the tub down, kicked off their moccasins, and ran into the shallow water.

Then they turned and scooped up handfuls of water to splash Ana and Francisca, who shrieked with laughter as the water hit them.

Finally, Ana scolded gently, "Now, girls, stop. We've come to wash the clothes that are in our baskets, *not* the ones we're wearing!"

As the sisters went to work, Josefina said, "The sun and the breeze will dry the clothes quickly today."

"Yes," agreed Ana. "Mamá would have said, 'You see, girls? God has sent us a good drying day. Monday is laundry day even in heaven.'"

"And then Mamá would have said, 'Pull your *rebozos* up to shade your faces, girls. You don't want your skin to look like old leather!'" added Francisca as she adjusted her shawl on her head. Francisca was always careful of her skin.

The sisters laughed softly and then grew quiet. Speaking of their mamá always made them thoughtful. Mamá had died the year

rebozo

before. The sorrow of her death was always in their hearts.

Josefina looked at the stream flowing past and listened to its low, rushing sound. Since Mamá died she had learned a truth that was both bitter and sweet. She had learned that love does not end. Josefina would always love Mamá, and so she would always miss her.

Josefina knew her sisters were also thinking about Mamá because Francisca said, "Look. See those yellow flowers across the stream?" She pointed with a soapy hand. "Aren't they primroses? Mamá used to love those."

"Yes, she did," said Clara, agreeing with Francisca for once. "Why don't you pick some, Josefina? You could dry them and put them in your memory box."

"All right," said Josefina. Papá had given her a little wooden box of Mamá's. Josefina called it her memory box because in it she kept small things that reminded her of Mamá.

The quickest, driest way to the primroses was to walk across a fallen log that made a narrow bridge over the stream. Josefina climbed up onto the log. She held her arms out for balance and began to walk across.

"Oh, do be careful," warned Ana.

Josefina did not think of herself as a brave person at all. She was afraid of snakes and lightning and guns, and shy of people she didn't know. But she wasn't afraid of crossing the log, which wasn't very high above the stream anyway. She walked across, picked the primroses, and tucked the stems in her pouch. On the way back, she decided to tease Ana to make her laugh. She pretended to lose her balance. She waved her arms wildly up and down and wobbled more and more with each step.

"Josefina Montoya!" said Ana, who saw that she was fooling. "How can you be so shy and sweet in company when you're so playful with your sisters? You tease the life out of me. You'll make me old before my time!"

"You sound just like our grandfather," said Josefina. She pretended to talk like Abuelito. "Yes, yes, yes, my beautiful granddaughters! This was the finest trip I've ever made! Oh, the adventures, the adventures! But this was my last trip. Oh, how these trips age me! They make me—"

"Old before my time!" all the sisters sang out together. Abuelito said the same thing after every journey.

Abuelito was their mamá's father. He was a trader, and once each year he organized a huge caravan. The caravan was made up of many carts pulled by oxen and many mules carrying packs. The carts and mules were loaded with wool, hides, and blankets in New Mexico. Then the caravan traveled more than a thousand miles south to Mexico City on a trail called the *Camino Real*.

When Abuelito got to Mexico City, he traded the goods he'd brought from New Mexico for things from all over the world. He traded for silk and cotton fabrics and lace, for iron tools, paper, ink, books, fine dishes, coffee, and sugar. Then the caravan would load up and start the long trip back to New Mexico.

Abuelito had been gone for more than six months.

Josefina and her sisters were excited because they expected Abuelito's caravan to return any day now. Their rancho was always the caravan's last stop before the town of Santa Fe, where Abuelito lived.

"I can't wait until Abuelito comes!" said Josefina.

She thought that the arrival of the caravan was the most exciting thing that happened on the rancho. The wagons were full of treasures to be traded in Santa Fe. But the most important treasure the caravan brought was Abuelito himself, safe and sound and full of wonderful stories.

"I'm going to go on the caravan with Abuelito someday," said Francisca, dreamily swirling a shirt in the stream. "I'll see everything there is to see, and then I'll settle down and live in Mexico City with Mamá's sister, our Tía Dolores. I'm sure she lives in a grand house and knows all the most elegant people."

Clara rolled her eyes and scrubbed hard with her soap. "That's ridiculous," she said. "We hardly know Tía Dolores. We haven't seen her for the whole ten years she's been living in Mexico City."

Francisca smiled a superior smile. "I'm older than you are, Clara," she said. "I was nearly six when Tía Dolores left. I remember her."

"Well," said Clara tartly. "If *she* remembers *you*, I'm sure she won't want you to live with her!"

Francisca was about to say something sharp when Josefina piped up.

"Ana," said Josefina, trying to keep the peace, "what do you hope Abuelito will bring on the caravan?"

"Shoes for Juan and Antonio," Ana replied. She and her husband, Tomás, had two little boys—Josefina's beloved nephews.

"I hope he brings that plow Papá needs," said Clara. She was always practical.

"How dull!" said Francisca. "*I'm* hoping for some new lace."

"You think too much of how you look," said Clara.

Francisca smirked. "Perhaps *you* ought—" she began.

But Josefina interrupted again. "Well, I know one thing we *all* hope Abuelito will bring," she said cheerfully. "Chocolate!"

"Lots!" said Francisca and Clara. They spoke at exactly the same moment, which made them laugh at each other.

"You haven't said what you're wishing for," Ana said to Josefina. She was squeezing water out of a petticoat. "Perhaps you're hoping for a surprise."

"Perhaps," said Josefina, smiling.

The truth was, she didn't know how to name what she wished for. What she wanted most was for her sisters to be at peace with one another. She wanted the household

to be running smoothly, and Papá to be happy and laughing and making music again. She longed for life to be the
way it was when Mamá was alive.

Right after Mamá died, Josefina had felt that the world
should end. How could life go on for the rest of them
without Mamá? It had seemed wrong, even cruel somehow,
that nothing stopped. The sun rose and set. Seasons passed
from one to another. There were still chores to be done
every day. There were clothes to be washed, weeds to pull,
animals to be fed, socks to be mended. But as time went by,
Josefina began to see that the steady rhythm of life on the
rancho was her best comfort. Mamá seemed close by when
Josefina and her sisters were together doing the laundry or
mending or cooking or cleaning. The sisters tried hard to do
the chores the way that Mamá had taught them. Every day,
they tried to remember their prayers and their manners and
how to do things right. But it was not easy without Mamá's
loving guidance.

Josefina looked at the primroses in her pouch and
thought of Mamá. Mamá had such faith in them all! She
brought out the best in them. Now that she was gone, they
struggled. Francisca and Clara squabbled. Ana worried.
Josefina often felt lost and unsure. And Papá was very
quiet. He had given away his violin, so he never filled the
house with music anymore. Josefina sighed. She didn't see

how the caravan could bring anything to help them.

"Here comes a surprise," said Clara. "But not one you'll like, Josefina."

Josefina looked up. "Oh, no," she said.

It was a small herd of goats. They were coming down the hill to drink from the stream. Josefina disliked all goats and one goat in particular. The biggest, oldest, meanest goat was named Florecita. Florecita was a sneaky, nasty bully. She bit, she rammed, and she'd eat anything. Josefina was afraid of her. She frowned when she spotted Florecita at the edge of the herd, heading straight for her.

Josefina backed away. She'd been poked by Florecita's sharp horns before, and she had no wish to be poked again. She scrambled up and stood on the log over the stream. Still Florecita did not stop coming. Josefina took one backward step, then another, then *SPLASH*! She missed her footing and fell off the log into the stream. It was very shallow, so she landed hard on the bottom.

"Oh, no!" she wailed. She saw that all but one sprig of the primroses had fallen out of her pouch. The flowers were floating on the water. Florecita snatched them up in her mean-looking teeth. She chewed them, looking satisfied. Then the goat turned and sauntered off to rejoin the herd.

"Are you all right?" Ana asked kindly as she helped

Josefina to her feet. "You really must not let Florecita bully
you like that!"

Josefina wrung out her skirt and smiled. "I tried to
stand up to Florecita," she joked, "but I ended up sitting
down, didn't I?"

She laughed along with her sisters, but she was annoyed
with Florecita. She was even more annoyed with herself for
letting Florecita scare her. As she looked at the one sprig of
primroses left in her pouch, she thought of another thing
she wanted that the caravan could not possibly bring her—
the courage to stand up to Florecita!

Abuelito's Surprise

The afternoon sun was so strong that it made the ground shimmer. Josefina dipped the drinking gourd into the water jar and took a long drink. Like everyone else on the rancho, she was up earlier than usual after her *siesta*, the midday rest. Papá had heard that the caravan would arrive this afternoon! Everyone was eagerly bustling about, preparing for its arrival.

Josefina poured some water into her cupped hand and held it to her face, cooling first one cheek and then the other. Then she opened her hand and let the water fall on a small cluster of flowers below. Mamá had planted these flowers, which grew in a protected corner of the back courtyard. With Josefina at her side, Mamá had tended her flowers with great devotion. She started them from seeds sent to her from Mexico City by her sister, Tía Dolores. Josefina remembered how pleased Mamá had always been when the caravan brought her some seeds from Tía Dolores. It had always seemed like a miracle to Josefina that the small brown seeds could, with water and Mamá's care, grow into beautiful, colorful flowers. Since Mamá died, Josefina had cared for the flowers by herself as best she could. Just now she sprinkled the rest of the water in the drinking gourd on them.

"I'm glad you remember to water your mamá's flowers, Josefina." Josefina turned and saw Papá. "Things grew well for your mamá, didn't they," Papá added.

"Yes, Papá," Josefina answered. "Mamá loved her flowers."

"So she did," said Papá, dipping the drinking gourd into the water jar. "And I hear Florecita likes flowers, too."

Josefina blushed.

"Don't worry," said Papá. "You'll stand up to Florecita when you're ready."

Josefina grinned a little bashfully. She watched Papá drink his water. Papá was tall and his eyebrows were so thick that he looked fierce until you saw the kindness in his eyes. All the sisters were respectful and rather shy of Papá. He had always been saving of his words, but since Mamá died he'd become especially quiet. Josefina knew his silence didn't come from sternness or anger. It came from sadness. She knew because she often felt the same way.

Mamá used to say that Josefina and Papá were alike.

They were both quiet, except with their family, but full of
ideas inside! Papá didn't have Mamá's easy manner with
people. It had always been Mamá who remembered the
names of everyone in the village, from the oldest person to
the newest baby. She remembered to ask if an illness was
better, or how the chickens were laying. She gave advice on
everything from growing squash to dyeing wool. Mamá
was well loved and well respected. She was Papá's partner.
She ran the household while he ran the rancho. Josefina
knew that Papá missed Mamá with all his heart.

Papá tipped the gourd so that the last drops of water
fell on the flowers. He smiled at Josefina, and then strode
off out the gate toward the fields.

Josefina carried the water jar to the kitchen.

"Oh, there you are, Josefina," said Ana. Her hands were
covered with flour, so she had to use the back of her wrist
to brush the sweat off her forehead. The heat of the cooking
fires was making her face red and her hair stick out. Pots
full of delicious-smelling concoctions sizzled, steamed, and
burbled over the fires.

There was always a big party with music and dancing, called a *fandango*, in the evening after the caravan
arrived. Neighbors from the little village nearby, friends
from the Indian *pueblo*, and all the people traveling with
the caravan were invited. Josefina could see that Ana was

overwhelmed with the preparations even though Carmen, the cook, was helping her. Two other servants were making *tortillas* as quickly as they could. Francisca and Clara were helping, too. They were peeling, chopping, and stirring as fast as their hands could move.

"Thank you for the water," said Ana. She handed Josefina a large basket. "Now please go to the kitchen garden and get me some onions."

"I'll come, too," Francisca said. "We need tomatoes."

The kitchen garden was just outside the back courtyard. Josefina gathered a basketful of onions and stood up. "Listen," she said to Francisca. Josefina could hear the rumble and squeak of wooden wheels that meant only one thing: The caravan was coming!

The girls smiled at each other, grabbed their baskets, and ran as fast as they could to the kitchen. "The caravan! It's coming!" they shouted. "Ana! Clara! It's coming!" They dropped their baskets outside the kitchen door as Clara rushed out to join them.

The three girls dashed across the courtyard, flew up the steps of the tower, and looked out the narrow window.

At first, all they saw was a cloud of dust stirring on the road from the village. Then the sound of the wheels grew louder and louder. Soon they heard the jingle of harnesses, dogs barking, people shouting, and the village church bell ringing. Next they saw soldiers coming over the hill with the sun glinting on their buttons and guns. Then came mule after mule carrying heavy packs strapped to their backs. Josefina counted thirty carts pulled by plodding oxen. The carts lumbered along on big wooden wheels. And there were so many people! Too many to count! There were cart drivers, traders, and herders driving sheep, goats, and cattle. People from the village and Indians from the nearby pueblo walked along with the caravan to welcome it.

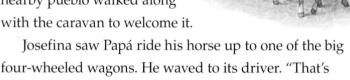

Josefina saw Papá ride his horse up to one of the big four-wheeled wagons. He waved to its driver. "That's Abuelito!" Josefina cried. "Look! Papá is greeting him."

Francisca leaned forward. "Who's that tall woman sitting next to Abuelito?" she wondered aloud. "She's greeting Papá as if she knows him."

But Josefina and Clara had already turned away from the window. They hurried down from the tower. Josefina ran to the kitchen and stuck her head in the door. "Come on," she said to Ana. "Papá and Abuelito are on their way up to the house."

"Oh dear," fussed Ana. "There's still so much to do. I'll never be ready for the fandango."

When Papá led Abuelito's big wagon up to the front gate, Josefina was the first to run out and greet it. Francisca, Clara, and Ana were close behind. Josefina thought she'd never seen a sight as wonderful as Abuelito's happy face. He handed the reins to the woman next to him and climbed down.

"My beautiful granddaughters!" said Abuelito. He kissed them as he named them. "Ana, and Francisca! Clara, and my little Josefina! Oh, God bless you! It is good to see you. This was the finest trip I've ever made! Oh, the adventures! But I'm getting too old for these trips. They make me old before my time. This is my last trip. My last."

"Oh, Abuelito!" said Francisca, taking his arm and laughing. "You say that every time!"

Abuelito threw back his head and laughed, too. "Ah, but this time I mean it," he said. "I've brought a surprise for you." He turned and held out his hand to the tall woman on the wagon. "Here she is, your Tía Dolores. She has come back to live with her mamá and me in Santa Fe. Now I have no reason to go to Mexico City ever again!"

Josefina and her sisters looked so surprised, Papá and

Abuelito laughed at them. Tía Dolores took Abuelito's hand and gracefully swung herself down from the wagon seat.

Papá smiled at her. "You see, Dolores? You have surprised my daughters as much as you surprised me," he said. "Welcome to our home."

"Gracias," Tía Dolores answered. She smiled at Papá and then she turned to the sisters. "I've looked forward to this moment for a long time," she said. "I've wanted to see all of you—my dear sister's children!"

She spoke to each one in turn. "You're very like your mamá, Ana," she said. "And Francisca, you've grown so tall and beautiful! Dear Clara, you were barely three when I left. Do you remember?"

Tía Dolores took Josefina's hand in both of her own. She bent forward so that she could look closely at Josefina's face. "At last I meet you, Josefina," she said. "You weren't even born when I left. And look! Here you are! Already a lovely young girl!" Tía Dolores straightened again. Her eyes were bright as she looked at all the sisters. "I'm so happy to see you all. I always loved hearing Abuelito's stories about you and the rancho. It's good to be back."

The girls were still too surprised to say much, but they smiled shyly at Tía Dolores. Ana was the first to collect herself. "Please, Abuelito and Tía Dolores. Come inside and have a cool drink. I'm sure you're tired and thirsty."

"I've looked forward to this moment for a long time," Tía Dolores said. "I've wanted to see all of you—my dear sister's children!"

She led Tía Dolores inside the gate. "You must excuse us, Tía Dolores," she said. "We haven't prepared a place for you to sleep."

"Goodness, Ana!" said Tía Dolores. "You didn't know I was coming. I didn't know myself, really, until the last minute. I've been caring for my dear aunt in Mexico City all these years. Bless her soul! She died this past spring, just before Abuelito's caravan arrived. I had no reason to stay. So I joined the caravan to come home."

"Yes," Abuelito said to the girls. "Your grandmother will be so pleased! Wait till Dolores and I get to Santa Fe the day after tomorrow! What a surprise, eh?"

Josefina could not take her eyes off Tía Dolores as everyone sat down together in the family *sala*. The room's thick walls and small windows kept it cool even in the heat of the afternoon.

Francisca whispered, "Isn't Tía Dolores's dress beautiful? Her sleeves must be the latest style from Europe."

But Josefina hadn't noticed Tía Dolores's sleeves, or anything else about her clothes. *This is Tía Dolores*, she kept thinking. *This is Mamá's sister.*

Josefina studied Tía Dolores to see if she looked like Mamá. Mamá had been the older of the two sisters, but Tía Dolores was taller. She didn't have Mamá's soft, rounded beauty, Josefina decided. Everything about Tía Dolores was sharper somehow. Her hands were bigger. Her face was narrower. Her voice didn't sound like Mamá's, either. Mamá's voice was high and breathy, like notes from a flute. Tía Dolores's voice was as low and clear as notes from a harp string. But when Tía Dolores laughed, Josefina was startled. If Josefina closed her eyes, it might be Mamá laughing.

There was a great deal of laughter in the family sala that afternoon as Abuelito told the story of his trip. Josefina sat next to Abuelito, her arms wrapped around her knees. She was happy. It reminded her of the old days to sit with her family this way and listen to Abuelito tell about his adventures.

"This was the most remarkable trip I've ever had," said Abuelito. "Oh, the trip to Mexico City was dull enough. But on the way home! Bless my soul! What an adventure! We were in terrible danger. Terrible! And your Tía Dolores saved us."

"Oh, but I didn't—" Tía Dolores began.

"No, my dear daughter! You *did* save us," said Abuelito. He turned to Papá and the girls. "You see," he said, "I was so glad that Dolores was going to come home with me. I finished all my business in Mexico City as quickly as I could. All went well until the day I came to Dolores's house to load up her belongings. Then the trouble began." He lowered his voice, pretending he did not want Tía Dolores to hear. "I had forgotten how stubborn your Tía Dolores is. What did she insist that we bring? You'll never guess! Her piano!"

Amazed, the girls all repeated, "Her *piano*?"

"Yes!" said Abuelito, pleased to have astonished them. "Such fuss and trouble! I told her it was too heavy and too big! But she said she'd sooner leave all her other belongings than her piano. So I grumbled, but I allowed the piano to be packed and loaded onto one of my wagons. We left Mexico City, and I complained about the piano every mile of the way." He shook his head. "Your Tía Dolores never said a word. She just let me go on and on, complaining. Well, then we came to Dead Man's Canyon. And do you know what happened?"

"What?" asked the girls.

"Thieves!" cried Abuelito in a voice so loud the girls jumped. "Thieves attacked the caravan! Oh, you've never seen such a fight! Shouting, swordfights, gunshots! The wagon with the piano was just behind ours. We saw two thieves climb up on it and push the driver off. Then six or seven of our men rushed over and wrestled with the two thieves, trying to pull them off the wagon. With all the yelling and fighting, the oxen harnessed to that wagon were scared. They bumbled into each other trying to get away. The wagon lurched forward, right to the edge of a deep gully. And then *crash*! Over it fell! Into the gully!"

The girls gasped.

Abuelito put his hand on his heart. "God bless us and save us all! What a sound that piano made when it fell!" he said. "A thud, and then a hollow *BOOM* that rumbled like musical thunder! It sounded like a giant had strummed all the keys in one stroke. The terrible sound bounced off the walls of Dead Man's Canyon. It seemed to grow louder with every echo. The thieves were terrified! They'd never heard such a sound in all their lives. Well! Didn't they take off as if they were on fire? All of them ran away as fast as their thieving legs could carry them! I'll bet they are still running!"

Everyone laughed. Abuelito laughed most of all, remembering with pleasure how frightened the thieves were. When he stopped laughing, he said, "After that, I put the piano in my own wagon. I never complained again. And so you see! Dolores did save us all, by insisting that we bring her piano."

"Well done, Dolores!" said Papá.

"But Abuelito," said Josefina, "was the piano hurt?"

Tía Dolores answered. "No, child," she said. "One leg is splintered, and the top is scratched. But I think it will sound fine."

"Oh," Josefina blurted, "may we see it?"

"No, no, no," said Abuelito. "It's too much trouble to open the crate. You'll just have to come to Santa Fe sometime to hear your aunt play."

Papá cleared his throat. "The girls and I have never seen or heard a piano," he said. "May I open the crate? I'll close it up afterward."

Tía Dolores turned to Abuelito. "Please," she said. "I'd like the girls to hear the piano."

Abuelito laughed and shrugged. "Of course, my dear, of course!" he said. "How can I say no to you after you saved my caravan?"

Tía Dolores kissed him. Then she and Papá led the girls outside to the wagon. Papá pried a few boards off the piano crate. Tía Dolores climbed into the wagon. She reached into the crate and pushed back the lid that protected the piano's keys. She didn't have much room to move her hands, but she played a chord. And then, as Papá and the four girls listened, she played a spirited tune.

Josefina felt the music thrum through her whole body. She had never before heard music like the piano's. The notes were so full, so perfect and delicate, that Josefina imagined she could almost see them as they filled the air. As Josefina listened, she realized that, through the music, Tía Dolores was telling them how happy she was. The music expressed her happiness better than words ever could, because it made all of them hearing it happy, too. Josefina stood still, barely breathing, listening hard until Tía Dolores stopped.

"Oh, dear," said Tía Dolores. "I'm afraid the piano's a little out of tune and I'm a little out of practice." Gently, she closed the lid over the keys.

Josefina wanted very much to touch the piano keys. She wanted to make the wonderful music happen herself. But she was too shy to ask Tía Dolores, so she said nothing.

"Gracias, Dolores," said Papá as he helped her climb down from the wagon.

"Oh, yes, gracias," said Ana, Francisca, and Clara.

"You must all come to see me in Santa Fe," said Tía Dolores, smiling. "I'll play for you, and show you how to play the piano yourselves."

The three oldest sisters followed Tía Dolores back inside the house. But Josefina stood next to the wagon until Papá had finished closing the crate. She knew she'd never forget the way Tía Dolores's music had sounded, or the way it had made her feel.

Papá said, "You liked the piano music, didn't you?"

"Oh, yes, Papá," answered Josefina. "I didn't want Tía Dolores to stop."

Papá smiled. "I didn't either," he said. "It made me miss playing my violin. Well, there will be plenty of fiddle music at the fandango tonight. You'd better go and get ready. The guests will be coming soon."

"Yes, Papá," Josefina answered. She took one last look at the piano crate and then started back inside. As she walked, she thought, *I wish there was some way I could let Tía Dolores know how much I loved the piano music. I wish I could give her something in return. But what?*

Later, when Josefina walked into the back courtyard, she knew the answer to her question. She thought of a fine gift to give Tía Dolores. *I'll give it to her during the fandango tonight,* she decided. She was pleased with her idea. She thought Tía Dolores would be pleased, too.

A Gift for Tía Dolores

T he sun set. Cool evening air slid down from the mountains, bringing darkness with it. Small bonfires were lit in the front courtyard for light and for warmth. As she crossed the courtyard, Josefina could hear Ana and Carmen thanking some neighbors who had come early with dishes of food for the fandango. No one noticed Josefina slip into the kitchen. She took a small water jar and slipped out again.

In the back courtyard, Josefina knelt in front of Mamá's flowers. One by one, she picked all the freshest flowers and put them in the water jar. Josefina was careful to break the flowers off near the ground so that the stems were long, but she didn't disturb the roots. There were not very many flowers, so Josefina had to pick almost all of them to have a bouquet beautiful enough to give to Tía Dolores.

The corner looked bare when she was through. *It's all right*, she told herself. *Mamá would approve. After all, Tía Dolores was the one who sent Mamá the seeds, so Tía Dolores should be the one to enjoy the flowers.*

Josefina straightened the flowers in the water jar. The

bouquet looked scrawny somehow, so
Josefina tied her blue hair ribbon around
the flowers in a big bow. *There!* she thought
with satisfaction. *That looks much better.*

She wanted the bouquet to be a surprise
for everyone, so she looked around for a place
to hide it. She had just entered the narrow passageway
between the front and back courtyards when she bumped
into Papá.

"What's this you've got here?" asked Papá, peering at
Josefina over the tops of the flowers.

"It's . . . they're a gift for Tía Dolores," explained Josefina.
"I wanted to give her something to thank her for the music."

It was too dark to see Papá's face clearly, but Josefina
could tell by his voice that he was smiling. "I think that's
a very fine idea," he said. "I'll tell you what. I'm going to
make a formal introduction of Tía Dolores to all our friends
and neighbors at the fandango tonight. After I do, perhaps
you will give Tía Dolores the bouquet."

"Yes, I will!" said Josefina happily.

"Very well," said Papá. "It will be our secret until then."

"Gracias, Papá," said Josefina. After Papá left, Josefina
put the jar of flowers under the bench in the passageway.
No one would see it there, and she would be able to fetch it
quickly when it was time to give it to Tía Dolores.

✱

More guests arrived every moment. They called out a chorus of greetings to each other as they crossed the front courtyard to the *gran sala*, the family's finest room. Because this was a very special night, the gran sala was lit with candles. Their wavering light made the guests' shadows swoop and dance on the walls.

Soon the musicians struck up a lively tune on their fiddles and the real dancing began. It seemed to Josefina that the dancers flew around the room with as much ease as their shadows had. Their feet hardly seemed to touch the floor at all as they whirled by in a blur of bright colors.

No one whirled faster than Francisca. No one looked happier or more beautiful. In the candlelight, her dark curly hair seemed to shine like a black stone in the stream. And Josefina was glad to see that Ana had put her responsibilities aside for a while and was dancing with her husband, Tomás. All around the sides of the gran sala, older ladies sat holding babies on their laps so that the babies' young mothers could dance. The old ladies clapped the babies' hands in time to the music.

Josefina and Clara were still too young to be allowed to dance, so they stood outside in the courtyard and leaned on the windowsill, looking in at the dancers. Josefina's feet danced along to the music. It was impossible to be still!

The music seemed to twist and turn in the air, wind its way around all the dancers, and find its way outside to tickle Josefina's feet so that they just had to move.

Every once in a while, over the music and conversation, Josefina and Clara could hear Abuelito's voice saying, "*BOOM!* What a sound! Those thieves ran off and I'll bet they're running still." Clara and Josefina grinned at each other. Abuelito was telling the story about Tía Dolores's piano over and over again. The girls noticed that the number of thieves grew larger every time Abuelito told the story!

The person both girls liked best to watch was Tía Dolores. She was easy to pick out of the crowd. "She dances well, doesn't she?" said Clara as Tía Dolores swept by.

"Yes," said Josefina. "She's as graceful as . . . as the music."

Soon Papá came by the window and nodded to Josefina. Josefina nodded back.

"What's that about?" asked Clara.

"It's a surprise," said Josefina, excited and smiling. "Stay here and you'll see."

She scurried across the courtyard to the passageway where she'd left the bouquet. It was very dark. Josefina bent down and felt under the bench for the water jar with the bouquet in it. It wasn't there.

That's odd, she thought.

Josefina stood up, perplexed. And then she saw the jar. It was lying on its side near one wall. It was empty.

Where is the bouquet? Josefina wondered anxiously.

She looked around the dark passageway. The bouquet was nowhere to be seen, but an odd white shape looming in the back courtyard caught her eye. She walked toward it and gasped.

Oh, no! The white shape was Florecita! The goat must have broken out of her pen and found her way into the back courtyard.

Josefina did not want to put Florecita back in her pen by herself. When she turned to go get help, she stepped on something. She stooped down and picked it up. At first she didn't know what it was. And then she saw. It was a few stems held together by a trampled, mud-stained blue ribbon.

Suddenly, Josefina realized what had happened. *Florecita had eaten the bouquet!* This was all that was left of the beautiful flowers that Josefina had picked for Tía Dolores.

But that was not the worst of it. At that
instant, Josefina saw what Florecita was
doing. Calm as could be, Florecita was
standing in the middle of what used to be
Mamá's flower garden, chewing a mouthful of stems. One hollyhock, root and all,
dangled from her mouth. Josefina could see
that almost no other flowers were left in the garden. Most
of what remained were scraggly, chewed, crushed, and
broken stems and a scattering of leaves and petals.

Florecita turned her yellow eyes on Josefina. The goat
looked very satisfied with herself.

Josefina was furious. "Florecita!" she hissed in a fero-
cious whisper. "You awful, awful animal! You've ruined
everything."

Josefina was so angry that she forgot to be afraid of
Florecita. She marched right up to the goat and yanked the
hollyhock out of her mouth. Florecita looked surprised. She
looked even more surprised when Josefina swatted her on
the back with the stems, saying, "How could you? You ate
the bouquet and you killed Mamá's flowers. Oh, I *hate* you,
Florecita!"

Josefina shoved Florecita hard. Then she took hold of
one of Florecita's fearsome horns and pulled with all her
strength. "Come with me!" she said.

Josefina dragged Florecita to her pen. She slammed the gate shut. "I hate you, Florecita," she said again. "I'll hate you forever!"

Josefina ran all the way back to the bench in the passageway and slumped down on it. There was nothing to be done. She looked at the dirty blue ribbon and the chewed stems wilting in her hand and fought back tears of disappointment.

"Josefina?" a voice said. "What are you doing here in the dark?"

Josefina looked up. Tía Dolores was coming toward her. Josefina could hardly talk. She showed the sad-looking stems to Tía Dolores. "This was a bouquet for you," she said in a shaky voice. "But our goat Florecita found it and ate it. And she killed Mamá's flowers, too."

"Ah," said Tía Dolores. She sat next to Josefina on the bench.

Slowly, Josefina explained. "I wanted to give you a gift to thank you for the piano music," she said. "So I picked all the best flowers. I tied my hair ribbon around them. The flowers were so pretty. They grew from the seeds you sent Mamá. I've been watering them since Mamá died, because I know she loved them. Now there are almost none left. Most of the flowers are dead."

Tía Dolores was a good listener. She sat still and gave

Josefina her full attention. The fandango seemed far away.
When Josefina was finished explaining, Tía Dolores said,
"Show me your mamá's flowers."

Josefina led Tía Dolores to the corner of the back courtyard. "You see," she said. "There's nothing left."

Tía Dolores knelt down. She looked at what was left of
the flowers. She scooped up a handful of soil and rubbed it
between her fingers. Gently, she touched the short, bitten-
off stems.

Then she smiled at Josefina. "Don't worry," she said.
"Your mamá planted these flowers well. The roots are deep
and strong. You've kept them healthy by watering the soil.
They'll live, I promise." She stood and brushed the soil off

her hands. "Do you like caring for flowers?" she asked.

Josefina nodded. "I used to help Mamá," she said.

"I brought some seeds with me when I left Mexico City," said Tía Dolores. "Perhaps you and I can plant them tomorrow."

"Oh, could we?" said Josefina.

"Yes," said Tía Dolores. "We'll wash your hair ribbon, too. Now we had better go back to the gran sala."

Papá met them at the door. "Josefina," he said, "where have you been? I introduced Tía Dolores, but then I couldn't find you."

"Oh, Papá," said Josefina. "Florecita ate the bouquet! And then she almost ruined all the rest of Mamá's flowers."

"Ah, that's too bad," said Papá sadly. He looked around the courtyard. "Is Florecita loose?"

"No," said Josefina. "I dragged her back to her pen and shut the gate."

"You did?" asked Papá. "But I thought you were afraid of Florecita."

"I am," said Josefina. "I mean, I was. I guess just now I was so angry at Florecita I forgot I was afraid!"

Papá laughed. "Well, we never know where our courage is going to come from!" he said. "I am sorry about the flowers, though."

"Tía Dolores says the flowers will be all right," Josefina

said to Papa. "She's going to help me plant new seeds tomorrow."

"Is she?" said Papá. He turned and smiled at Tía Dolores. "Well, then, Dolores," he said, "that means you'll have to come back often. You'll have to visit us to see how the flowers are coming along."

"I will," said Tía Dolores. "God willing."

"Come inside and have something to eat now," said Papá. "Ana would never forgive us if we didn't enjoy the food she's prepared."

Josefina followed Papá and Tía Dolores into the gran sala. She grinned to herself. *I guess the caravan didn't need to bring me the courage to stand up to Florecita after all,* she thought. *It turns out I already had it. But I might never have found out if I hadn't picked a bouquet for Tía Dolores.*

An idea danced through Josefina's head just then. As quick as the flicker of starlight on water, the idea appeared and disappeared. But it was an idea that would come again and again all the rest of the night and through the next day, until it grew from an idea into a heartfelt hope.

Josefina's Idea

t breakfast Tía Dolores said, "I want to see as much of the rancho as I can today."

So after breakfast Josefina led Tía Dolores through the orchard, past the cornfields, and to the stream. They filled water jars and carried them up to water the kitchen garden. Then they picked some fat pumpkins for Tía Dolores to take home with her to Santa Fe the next day. "I am sure my mother has no pumpkins as big as these in her garden!" said Tía Dolores.

Wherever she went, Tía Dolores found something to praise. Josefina led Tía Dolores to the weaving room. There Clara showed her the sheep's wool she had carded, spun, and dyed. Tía Dolores admired the colors. "There are no colors finer than these in all of Mexico," she said.

Tía Dolores was a good teacher. She showed Clara a faster way to knit the heel on a sock. She showed Francisca how to sew a patch over a hole so that it hardly showed at all.

Josefina was in the back courtyard clearing away the

dead stems Florecita had trampled when Tía Dolores joined her.

"I've brought you some seeds to plant," she said to Josefina as she handed her a small package.

"Gracias!" said Josefina.

"I'll help you for a while. Then I promised Ana I would make bread with her," said Tía Dolores. She began to dig holes in the soil for the seeds. "Ana has lots of responsibilities, doesn't she?"

"Yes," agreed Josefina. "It's hard for Ana. Mamá ran the household so smoothly. But Ana doesn't always know what to do, and Mamá is not here to teach her."

"Ana is young," said Tía Dolores as she covered some seeds with soil. "It's a good thing she has you and Francisca and Clara to help her."

Josefina nodded slowly. "We try," she said. "But sometimes..." She stopped and dug a little hole in the soil.

Tía Dolores gave her a questioning look.

Josefina sighed. "You see," she said, "Francisca and Clara fight a lot. They are so different! Clara is careful and practical, and Francisca is quick and fiery. When Mamá was alive, she put a stop to their arguments before they began. But now... well, Ana tries, but she is too soft-hearted and they won't mind her. I try to joke them out of fighting, but it doesn't always work."

"'Blessed are the peacemakers,'" said Tía Dolores softly, "'for they will be called the children of God.'" She smiled at Josefina. "You know," she said, "it's perfectly natural for sisters to disagree. You should have heard your mamá and me sometimes! She was quite a few years older than I was. I'm sure she thought I was a miserable pest. I wanted to be like her. Once I wore her best sash without her permission, and I lost it. Your mamá was very angry. She wouldn't speak to me for days. But she finally forgave me."

Josefina realized suddenly, *Tía Dolores misses her sister. She misses Mamá, too, just as much as we do.* She said, "I wish you could be here to protect these flowers from Florecita when they bloom."

"I'd love to see the flowers," said Tía Dolores. "But *you* can protect them from Florecita. You aren't afraid of her anymore. You don't need me. You will make your mamá's flowers bloom again and keep them safe, Josefina. I know you will."

✿

When the afternoon had cooled into early evening, Tía Dolores and Abuelito walked to the village. They wanted to say a prayer at Mamá's grave. They were also going to visit Papá's oldest sister, who lived in the village.

Josefina and her sisters gathered in a corner of the front courtyard that was still warm from the heat of the day's sun. They were husking corn. Josefina said, "Hasn't it been nice today, having Tía Dolores here?"

"Yes!" said Ana. "She was such a help to me! And she was so kind to my little boys."

"Tía Dolores is a very sensible, hardworking person," said Clara. That was her highest praise.

"Oh, Clara!" protested Francisca. "You make her sound as dull as these ears of corn! I found her to be elegant and graceful."

Josefina decided the time had come to tell her sisters her idea. She picked up an ear of corn and peeled the husk slowly. "What if," she said quietly, "we asked Tía Dolores to stay? She could help us and teach us, the way she did today."

"She wouldn't stay," said Francisca. "She's used to life in Mexico City, where there are lots of grand people and grand houses. She doesn't want to live on a rancho."

"But she said she always loved to hear about the rancho when Abuelito came to visit her, remember?" said Josefina. "And she doesn't act fancy or put on airs. She likes it here. She was interested in everything."

"Yes," said Ana. "But I think perhaps she has come home hoping to get married and start a family of her own. She's not too old for that, you know."

"She wouldn't have to stay here forever," said Josefina.

Josefina picked up an ear of corn and peeled the husk slowly.
"What if," she said quietly, "we asked Tía Dolores to stay?"

"Just for a few months. And anyway, she is our aunt. We *are* her family."

"Well," said Clara in her flat, no-nonsense manner. "Even if Tía Dolores would be willing to stay, it wouldn't be proper for us to ask her. Papá would have to approve of the idea. He would have to be the one to ask her to stay."

Josefina's heart sank. She hadn't thought of that. She knew Clara was right.

"Who wants to be the one to present the idea to Papá?" Clara asked. "I certainly don't." She turned to Josefina. "It's your idea," she said. "Do you want to talk to Papá about it?"

Josefina looked down at the ear of corn in her hands. "No," she said in a small voice.

"Will you go to him, Ana?" Clara asked. "You are the oldest."

"Oh, I couldn't!" said Ana. "Papá might think I was complaining. If I say that I need Tía Dolores's help, he might think I don't want to do what it is my responsibility to do."

"Oh!" exclaimed Francisca. She stood up and brushed off her skirt. "*I'm* not afraid to talk to Papá. I'll just march right up to him and say, 'Papá! You must ask Tía Dolores to stay!'"

Ana, Clara, and Josefina looked at each other. They knew that was not at all the right way to speak to Papá! It wasn't that Papá was stern or cold. But he was the *patrón*, the head of the rancho and the head of their family. The girls had never presented such an important idea to him before. It would have to be done politely and with respect.

"Wait, Francisca!" said Josefina. "I think all of us should speak to Papá. We should go together. That way Papá will see that all four of us would like Tía Dolores to stay."

Ana and Clara didn't move.

"Come on," said Josefina. She grinned. "Don't worry. I'll do the talking if you don't want to. Last night I had the courage to stand up to Florecita. Papá is much, much kinder than *she* is!"

The sisters found Papá near the animal pens. He was tightening the latch on the gate.

He smiled when he saw Josefina. "The latch is stronger now," he said. "We shouldn't have any more goats in Mamá's flowers."

"That's good!" said Josefina. She swallowed. Francisca gave her a little shove forward. "Papá," Josefina said. "May we ask you something?"

Papá looked at the four girls. "Yes?" he said.

"Do you think," Josefina said carefully, "that you could ask Tía Dolores to stay here with us for a while?"

"Ask her to stay?" repeated Papá.

"Yes," said Josefina. "Not forever, just for a while. She could help us. And she could teach us, the way . . . the way

Mamá did. Please, would you ask her?"

Josefina saw a look of sadness cross Papá's face. He turned away. "I'll consider it," he said.

"But Papá," Francisca blurted. "You must—"

Josefina tugged on Francisca's sleeve and frowned at her to make her stop talking.

"Gracias, Papá," said Josefina. She hesitated, and then she added, "We need Tía Dolores."

Then she and her sisters left.

The next morning, all the girls were up early. Even Francisca, who was usually slow getting dressed, was ready and waiting with Ana, Clara, and Josefina next to Abuelito's wagon. They watched the servants load Abuelito's belongings onto the wagon.

Then, with sinking hearts, the sisters saw Tía Dolores's trunk loaded onto the wagon as well.

"Papá didn't ask her!" Francisca groaned.

"Or maybe he did, and she said no," said Ana.

"She doesn't want to stay," Clara added.

Josefina was so disappointed, she couldn't talk. A lump rose in her throat when she heard Papá and Tía Dolores and Abuelito coming. Suddenly, Josefina didn't want to stand there by the wagon one second longer. She couldn't bear to kiss Tía Dolores and Abuelito good-bye.

Without a murmur, she slipped away, back inside the house. She went to the gran sala because it was the only room that was sure to be empty. As she walked into the cool darkness of the gran sala, she remembered how it had looked the night of the fandango, full of life and music. Now there was nothing but shadows.

Then, in a corner of the room, Josefina saw a large, dark shape. She caught her breath when she saw what it was: Tía Dolores's piano! Instantly, Josefina knew what that meant. Tía Dolores would never have left her piano, unless . . .

Josefina flew across the courtyard and out the front gate so fast, it seemed as if she had wings on her feet.

Tía Dolores caught Josefina in her arms. "There you are, Josefina!" Tía Dolores said. "I wanted to say good-bye to you."

Josefina pulled back and looked at Tía Dolores's face.

"I'm going to Santa Fe," Tía Dolores said. "I'm going to see my dear mamá, whom I have not seen for ten years. But then I'll come back."

"When?" asked Josefina.

Tía Dolores laughed. "Soon," she said. "And when I come back, I'll stay as long as you need me."

Josefina hugged Tía Dolores hard. Then Tía Dolores swung herself up onto the wagon beside Abuelito.

"Well, well, well," said Abuelito. He pretended to be cross. "Now it seems that if I want to see Dolores, I'm going to have to come here and see all of you girls, too. What a bother!" He sighed. "At least I don't have to carry that piano with me today. Though if we meet up with any thieves, I'll just have to frighten them off with my singing, I suppose!"

Then he kissed Josefina and her sisters good-bye and gave them his blessing.

"*Adiós*, Abuelito!" called all the girls as the wagon pulled away. "Adiós, Tía Dolores."

"Come back soon!" Josefina sang out as she waved good-bye.

As soon as the wagon was out of sight, Josefina hurried back inside. She went to the kitchen to get a jar for water to sprinkle on Mamá's flowers.

Tía Dolores will be back soon, she thought. *I want the flowers to be beautiful when she returns!*

Josefina set off for the stream, humming a happy tune.

Light and Shadow

The month that Tía Dolores was away visiting her parents in Santa Fe felt very long to Josefina. She missed her aunt every minute that she was gone. But Tía Dolores kept her promise, and she returned to the rancho, just in time to help with the October harvest.

One rainy night, two weeks after Tía Dolores had come back, Josefina and her sisters were sewing in front of the fire in the family sala. "María Josefina Montoya," Tía Dolores said, "how beautiful you look in your new dress!"

Josefina blushed and smiled at her aunt. "Gracias," she replied.

Tía Dolores had given Josefina and each of her sisters some material. Josefina's material was a pretty yellow, with narrow stripes and tiny berries on it. She had cut her material carefully, the way Mamá had taught her. Then, stitch by tiny stitch, she had sewn her dress together all by herself. Now, as she spun around, the hearth fire cast a pattern of light and shadow swooping across the dress like a flock of fluttering birds.

Josefina stopped spinning and sighed with contentment.

She was grateful for the fire's warmth and cheerful brightness. A steady, heavy rain was falling outside, but inside it was cozy. The thick, whitewashed *adobe* walls kept out the cold and took on a rosy glow from the firelight.

Tía Dolores sat next to Clara. "Don't use such a long thread in your needle," she advised Clara gently. "It might tangle."

Josefina grinned. "Remember, Clara?" she said. "Mamá used to say, 'If you make your thread too long, the devil will catch on to the end of it!'"

All the sisters smiled and nodded, and Tía Dolores said, "I remember your mamá saying that to me when we were young girls learning to sew!"

Tía Dolores was smiling too. But Josefina saw that her eyes were sad, and she knew that Tía Dolores was missing Mamá.

Josefina and her sisters thought of Mamá every day. They tried to do their chores the way Mamá had taught them, and to be as respectful, hardworking, and obedient as she would have wished them to be. Often, they recalled her wise and funny sayings and songs. And every night, they remembered her in their prayers.

As Clara shortened her thread, she looked at Josefina's dress. "You'll get a lot of wear out of that dress," she said, sounding sensible as usual. "It was a good idea to make it too long. That way you can grow into it."

"Oh, dear!" said Josefina, looking at her hem. "Is my dress too long?"

"Not at all. It's perfect," said Ana in her kind way. "You've done a fine job, Josefina. And you are the first one of us to finish." Ana had not even begun her dress yet. She had decided to make vests for her two little boys first.

Francisca sighed a huge sigh. "I'm far from finishing my dress," she said. "I've still so much to do."

"You shouldn't have chosen such a fancy dress pattern," said Clara, pricking her material with the sharp needle.

Tía Dolores had given Francisca a sewing diary that showed all the latest styles from Mexico City, and the girls had each chosen a dress pattern to follow. Clara was making a dress that was plain and simple. She prided herself on being practical and often felt called upon to point it out when someone else wasn't. That someone was usually Francisca.

Francisca had chosen an elaborate pattern from the sewing diary. She'd begun enthusiastically. She cut into the material boldly, talking all the while about how splendid her dress would be. But the long, slow work of sewing the pieces together bored Francisca. She complained with every stitch. "I'll never finish my dress," she said now, "unless someone helps me with this endless stitching."

She glanced sideways at Tía Dolores.

Josefina saw the sideways look. She knew that Francisca wanted Tía Dolores to sew for her. But Tía Dolores calmly continued her own sewing. She said nothing, even when Francisca sighed loudly again. Josefina was not surprised. In the last two weeks, she had learned that Tía Dolores was always willing to give help and advice. But she would not do the girls' work for them.

A few days ago, Josefina and Tía Dolores had worked together in the corner of the back courtyard where Mamá's flowers grew. Tía Dolores showed Josefina how to prepare the flowers for the winter. She explained how to cut back the dead stems and cover the earth with leaves to protect it from ice and snow. She watched with care to be sure Josefina was doing everything correctly. Tía Dolores helped, but she made it clear that the flowers were Josefina's responsibility. "I want you to know how to care for them by yourself after I leave," she'd said. "I know you can do it. I have faith in you."

Tía Dolores worked hard teaching, and she expected the girls to work hard learning. "Our energies and abilities are gifts from God," she often said. "He means for us to put them to good use." Sometimes Josefina thought that perhaps Tía Dolores had too *much* faith in her abilities!

Francisca frowned and rustled her material. She made a

great show of holding it up to the fire and squinting as she stitched. Clara glanced at the hem Francisca was sewing. "Just look at the size of your stitches!" Clara said. "They're much too big."

"Oh, Clara!" said Francisca crossly. "The stitches are on the inside! No one will see them."

"Yes, they will!" said Josefina, who didn't like to hear her sisters squabble. "No one's dress swirls more than yours at a dance, Francisca. And no one is more admired!"

Josefina whirled around the room, pretending to be Francisca dancing. "See my hem stitches?" she asked. She sang a dancing song that had been one of Mamá's favorites, and soon her sisters joined her dancing.

Tía Dolores knew the song, too. She went straight to the piano and began to play it. She played so loudly and they were all singing and laughing and dancing so much that none of them heard the door open.

The next thing Josefina knew, Papá was there, tapping his foot in time to Tía Dolores's music. He watched the girls dance until the song was over. When they stopped, he folded his arms across his chest and pretended to scold. "Dancing instead of sewing?" he asked. He tried to look stern, but his eyes were full of fun. "Who started this fandango?"

"I did, Papá!" said Josefina, flushed and breathless.

"I was celebrating. I've finished my dress. I made it from material Tía Dolores gave to us."

"How thoughtful of her," said Papá. He turned to Tía Dolores. "You are very kind to my daughters. Gracias."

Tía Dolores looked pleased. "My father bought the material this summer from traders who came to Santa Fe from the United States. The traders brought all sorts of things to trade—tools and clothes, paper and ink—"

"And pretty material!" Josefina added happily.

"*Sí*," said Papá. "I know about the *americanos* and the trail they follow. They first came to Santa Fe three years ago. Before that, it was illegal for them to come to New Mexico." He looked thoughtful. "I hope that trading with the americanos will be a good thing. I've heard that the traders need pack mules, so I'm raising some to take to Santa Fe next summer. I'll sell or swap the mules to get tools and other things we need on the rancho. It should be a profitable business."

"Oh, Papá," Josefina asked, "may we go to Santa Fe with you next summer?"

"Perhaps," said Papá, smiling at her eagerness. "But right now, I think all of you girls had better go to bed. I'm going to the village."

"In this storm?" asked Ana.

"It's because of the storm that I'm going," said Papá

as he put on his hat. "I want to be sure Magdalena is all right." Tía Magdalena was Papá's sister. She was much older than he was, and she lived alone in the village about a mile from the rancho. "Her roof is not as strong as it should be, and her house is near the stream. I'm worried about flooding. Most of the time, nothing is more welcome than rain. But it's unusual for it to rain so late in the year, and such a hard rain can mean trouble."

Josefina listened. They'd been making so much noise, they hadn't noticed that the wind had an angry sound to it now, and the rain was coming down harder and harder. Josefina turned a worried face up to Papá.

"Now, now. There's no need for you to worry, Josefina," Papá said in his deep, comforting voice. "Our house is high above the stream. God will keep you safe, and Tía Dolores is here to look after you."

"Sí, Papá," said Josefina. "But if the stream floods—"

"Our harvest is safely in," said Papá. "We'll move the animals to higher ground if we need to. Now come and say good night to me before I go."

The girls knelt before Papá, the palms and fingers of their hands pressed together as for prayer. Papá gave each girl his blessing and kissed her praying hands. His smile was loving as he looked down on his daughters' upturned faces. "Go to bed," he said. "The sky will be blue tomorrow."

Tía Dolores opened the door for Papá. "God go with you," she said softly.

Papá nodded. Then he went out into the windy, rainy night.

Papá had told Josefina not to worry, but she could not obey. Moment by moment the wind grew wilder. It shrieked and howled and hurled the rain against the roof and the walls as if it were trying to destroy the house with its anger. Josefina listened, shivering. And so, when the church bell rang in the night, Josefina was already awake. The bell's fast *clang, clang, clang* meant *danger, danger, danger!*

"The church bell is ringing," said Josefina to Clara and Francisca. "Hurry! Get dressed. Papá may need our help."

The sisters dressed as fast as they could. Just as they were finishing, Tía Dolores came to fetch them. She was carrying a small candle. Her voice was calm and very serious. "Come, girls," she said. "We must save as much as we can from the kitchen garden."

Josefina, Clara, and Francisca followed Tía Dolores. They were still under the cover of the roof when suddenly, *CRACK!* Lightning split the sky. Josefina couldn't move. All her life she had feared lightning. Mamá had understood. She would hug Josefina to her and wrap her rebozo around both of them. She'd cover Josefina's eyes with her hand so

that Josefina wouldn't have to
see the wicked flash of light
or the plunge into darkness
that followed. She'd hold
Josefina so close that the
beating of her heart almost
blocked out the sound of the
thunder. *Mamá!* thought Josefina

now, bracing herself for another flash. *Help me!*

Just then, Josefina felt Tía Dolores put a strong arm
around her shoulders. Tía Dolores's little candle sputtered
wildly in the wind, but it didn't go out. By its feeble light,
Josefina saw Tía Dolores's gentle face. "Come with me,
Josefina," she said.

Josefina took a shaky breath. She leaned close to
Tía Dolores. Together, they stepped forward. Clara and
Francisca followed behind. The rain put the little candle
out. But Tía Dolores's step was sure, even in the darkness.
She led the girls across the front courtyard, through the
passageway, and into the back courtyard. As they passed
Mamá's flowers, Josefina remembered what Tía Dolores
had said when they'd worked together: *I know you can do
it. I have faith in you.*

Lightning sliced the sky and thunder boomed, again
and again. Josefina shuddered, but Tía Dolores's arm gave

her courage. She stayed within its safe hold as they went out the back gate to the kitchen garden.

Carmen, the cook, and her husband, Miguel, were already there, filling big baskets with squashes, beans, chiles, and pumpkins. The kitchen garden was awash in mud. It made Josefina sad to see it. She and her sisters had worked so hard all spring and summer tending the garden! She was sorry to pick the squashes that were not perfectly ripe yet, but she knew it was better than letting them be washed away or rot from lying in water.

And there was so *much* water! A river of it rushed through the center of the garden, and the rain was still falling in torrents. Mud pulled at Josefina's moccasins and splashed up onto her legs. Soon she was soaked to the skin. Her hands were numb with cold and caked with dirt. Her arms were tired from lifting mud-streaked pumpkins, and her back hurt from carrying her heavy basket. Lightning flashed all around her and thunder rumbled. But Josefina bent to her work, trying to ignore the force and fury of the storm.

Tía Dolores has faith in me, Josefina said to herself. *I can't let her down.*

Turning Blankets into Sheep

ust as Papá had promised, the sky was a clean, clear blue the next morning. Only a few gray clouds remained, and they scuttled across the horizon as if they were ashamed, shoving against each other in their hurry to get away. Below, the wet, shiny ground was crisscrossed everywhere with thin little rivers no bigger than trickles, trying to find their way down the hill back to the stream.

Papá had come home from the village at dawn, just in time for morning prayers. As she'd knelt in front of the altar in the family sala, Josefina had thanked God for Papá's safe return. When the family gathered in the kitchen for break-fast, Josefina saw that Papá looked tired. Tía Dolores gave him some mint tea. He sat down and took a long, grateful sip before he spoke.

"You all did a fine job of saving as much as you could from the garden," he said. "I'm afraid the news from the village is not as good. I was in time to save Magdalena's roof, but one whole corner of the church collapsed. Some of the villagers had not harvested yet, so their crops were swept away by the stream when it rose over its banks."

"What a blessing it is that you brought our harvest in early!" said Ana. "We'll be able to share it with the villagers who lost their crops. No one will go hungry this winter."

"Sí," said Papá. "That is a blessing. But we've suffered another loss. The shepherds were moving our sheep from their summer grazing lands in the mountains down to the winter pastures closer to the rancho. When the storm began, the shepherds took a shortcut to save time. Just as they were crossing the bottom of a deep *arroyo*, a flash flood came gushing through it. The water came so hard and so fast that the sheep couldn't get out of its way. The shepherds risked their lives to save as many sheep as they could. But hundreds of our sheep were drowned."

arroyo

Everyone was still. They looked at Papá, their faces full of concern. Then Josefina went to stand by Papá's side. She put her hand on his arm and he patted it while he stared into the fire. So many sheep killed! Josefina knew that this was a terrible disaster. How cruel the storm had been! The rancho could not survive without sheep. They provided meat, and wool for weaving and for trading. What would Papá do?

Papá's voice was heavy with discouragement. "The sheep

were very valuable," he said. "My father and grandfather built up the flocks over many years. It will take a long, long time for us to recover from this loss." He sighed. "We'll just have to start over. I'll have to trade the mules I was raising. I have nothing else to trade. I'll have to use the mules to get new sheep so that we can increase our flocks again."

"Perhaps not," said Tía Dolores. She'd been so quiet, they'd almost forgotten she was there. Now she spoke to Papá, respectfully but firmly. "Forgive me for speaking, but perhaps it won't be necessary to trade the mules. Perhaps you could use the old sheep to get new sheep."

They all stared at her. "Please go on," said Papá.

Tía Dolores explained. "The old sheep provided you with sacks and sacks of wool when they were sheared last spring," she said. "Your storerooms are full of their fleece. What if we used that wool to weave as many blankets as we can? We'll trade the blankets to the villagers for new sheep. We can trade with the Indians at the pueblo, too."

"But they all weave their own blankets," said Papá. "Why would they want more?"

"To trade to the americanos," answered Tía Dolores. "My father told me that the americanos are glad to trade their goods for blankets. They value the blankets for their warmth and strength and beauty."

"I don't understand," said Francisca. "Who will do all of this weaving you talk about?"

Tía Dolores smiled. "We will," she said. "You and your sisters and I. The household servants will weave, and any workers on the rancho who are able."

Josefina saw that Francisca wasn't pleased with this answer, and Clara and Ana looked unsure. But Papá seemed to be giving the idea grave consideration. "Trading blankets for sheep," he said thoughtfully. "Perhaps it would be good for both sides. Our neighbors would help us by giving us the sheep we need. And *we* would help *them* by weaving blankets they can trade for goods that they need."

"Sí," said Tía Dolores simply.

Ana nudged Josefina with her elbow and raised her eyebrows. None of the sisters had ever heard Papá discuss business with a woman before. He had never discussed business with Mamá. But Papá didn't seem to be offended by Tía Dolores's forwardness.

"But Tía Dolores!" Francisca protested. "I don't see how we can weave any more than we already do! We hardly have time to do all our household chores as it is."

"We'll get up earlier," said Tía Dolores briskly. "If all four of you help—"

"Josefina can't help," said Francisca. "She doesn't know how to weave."

"That's true," Clara said. "Mamá never taught her, because Josefina was too small. She's *still* too small to work the big loom."

"My servant, Teresita, weaves on a smaller loom that hangs from the ceiling," said Tía Dolores. "I'm sure she'd be willing to teach Josefina to weave on one like it. And I'm sure Josefina is big enough to do it. Josefina can help."

Josefina saw Papá looking at her. His smile said that he loved her even if he wasn't sure she could be of help with the weaving. With all her heart, Josefina wanted to please Papá. She could tell that Tía Dolores's idea had caught his interest and given him a little hope. And so she spoke up with spirit.

"I'd like to learn to use the small loom," she said. "And I can help wash and card and spin wool for the big loom. I know where to find the plants we use to make dye to color the wool, and . . . and Mamá always used to say that I was good at untangling knots."

Papá laughed out loud. His laugh was a sudden, unexpected, wonderful sound. "Well," he said to Tía Dolores. "If all of your weavers are as eager as my little Josefina, you'll turn the wool into blankets and the blankets into sheep in no time! I think we should give your plan a try."

Tía Dolores was pleased. "We will pray for God's help," she said, "as we put His gifts to good use. Won't we, girls?"

Her smile was so happy, so full of energy and encour-agement, that all the sisters—even Francisca—had to smile back and say, "Sí!"

❋

That very afternoon, Tía Dolores brought Josefina to Teresita. "Will you teach Josefina to weave?" she asked.

Teresita was working at a loom that hung near one wall and stretched from ceiling to floor. She looked at Josefina, and then she smiled. Teresita's smile seemed to use her whole face, because her eyes were surrounded by wrinkles of good humor. "Sí," she said.

"Gracias," said Tía Dolores. "You might as well begin right now. As I always say, 'The saints cry over lost time.'"

She left, and Teresita watched her go with a twinkle in her eye. Josefina could tell that she and Teresita were thinking the same thing—that Tía Dolores gave the saints very little reason to cry! She never wasted time!

That first day, Josefina had to do her row of weaving over and over again before it was smooth and even. But Teresita was very patient, and gradually Josefina's hands became accustomed to the feeling of the wool. When Josefina came for her next weaving lesson, Teresita had set up a loom for her to use by herself.

Josefina enjoyed her weaving lessons with Teresita. It was a pleasure to weave the wool through the strands, and

to push the newly woven row down so that it fit snugly next to the row below it. Part of the pleasure was knowing that with each row, Josefina was adding to a blanket that would help Papá replace the sheep he'd lost. Josefina was pleased and proud to be of help to her family. And as the days went by and she learned to be a better weaver, she was pleased and proud of herself for learning something new. *I may be the youngest and the smallest, but I can help, just like my sisters*, she thought. *I can help turn blankets into sheep! Tía Dolores was right.*

Rabbit Brush

F ollow me!" Josefina shouted happily. She ran up the hill as swift and light as a bird skimming over a stream. The air at the top smelled of spicy juniper and piney *piñón*. It was pure and cool and thin and sweet. Josefina turned around and called back to her sisters, "Wait till you see! There's *lots* of rabbit brush up here!"

Josefina and her sisters were on an expedition to gather wildflowers, herbs, roots, barks, berries, and leaves.

rabbit brush

They'd use them to make dyes to color the wool for weaving. They set to work gathering rabbit brush for yellow dye, delighted to be out in the bracing air and bright sunshine. The morning flew by, and later, at midday when the sun was hot and high, the sisters stopped for lunch. Josefina bit into a plum that was warm from the sunshine. The breeze lifted her hair off her back and cooled her face. "I wish Tía Dolores had been able to come with us today," she said. "She'd enjoy this."

✿

Tía Dolores had gone to the village. She was bringing food to some of the villagers who had lost their crops in the flood.

"Sí!" agreed Ana and Clara. Francisca had a mouthful of tortilla.

Josefina grinned. She took a sprig of rabbit brush out of her basket and pretended to be Tía Dolores. "We'll put these flowers to good use, won't we, girls?" she said, imitating Tía Dolores's energetic manner. Ana and Clara laughed, especially when Josefina put the flowers to good use tickling them!

But Francisca grabbed the flowers away. "Whenever Tía Dolores talks about putting things to good use, it always ends up meaning more work for us," she grumbled. "All this weaving, for example."

Josefina smiled. "I *like* the weaving," she said.

"Well," said Francisca. "It's new to you. But I find it very dull." She collapsed back on the grass and fanned herself with the sprig of flowers. "I'm worn out from it! Anyway, I thought that when Tía Dolores came, there would be *less* work for us, not *more*. But Tía Dolores is always at work. She's always trying to fix things and improve things and change things—especially *us*!" Francisca poked and prodded Clara's arm with the sprig of rabbit brush as she continued to complain. "Tía Dolores is always trying to poke and prod us into being different than we are. She's never satisfied. She always thinks we can be better."

"Tía Dolores is helping us by teaching us," said Ana.

"Tía Dolores's help is not *exactly* what I expected it to be," Francisca said. "Tía Dolores isn't, either. She seems different than she was when she came here the first time."

"Yes!" said Josefina. "Tía Dolores seems happier."

"She's letting her skin get rough and red," said Francisca, who was vain about her own complexion.

Josefina did not like to hear Francisca criticize their aunt. "Why are you speaking this way about Tía Dolores?" she asked Francisca. "You were the one who used to say that she was elegant and that her clothes were beautiful."

"She never wears those beautiful clothes anymore," said Francisca, "just everyday work clothes." She shook her head and said mournfully, "Soon, I expect none of us will have anything *but* worn-out work clothes because Tía Dolores is determined to weave all our wool into blankets. I'm sure she won't spare even enough for new sashes for us. Not that it matters how we look. We don't have time to do anything but work these days! We're up long before dawn—"

"Ah, that's it," said Ana. "You are out of sorts because you have to get up so early! Mamá always said no one has a sweeter temper than you do, Francisca—as long as you have plenty of sleep!"

Josefina noticed that when Ana mentioned Mamá, a strange look crossed Francisca's face. Francisca started to say something, but then she changed her mind.

Josefina took hold of Francisca's hand and swung it as they walked together, heading home after lunch. "Remember the morning song Mamá used to sing to you to help you wake up?" she asked Francisca.

Ever so briefly, the strange look crossed Francisca's face again. Then she began to sing, "Arise in the morning..." She stopped. "How did it go?" she asked. "I've forgotten. Sing it for me, Josefina."

Josefina began to sing:

> *Here comes the dawn,*
> *now it gives us the light of day.*
> *Arise in the morning*
> *and see that day has dawned.*

Josefina sang the song in her clear, sweet voice as the girls made their way down the hill. Tía Dolores met them as they passed the orchard. She was carrying a basket full of apples, walking with her usual purposeful stride. Wisps of her ruddy auburn hair curled out from under her rebozo, and her skirt flapped in the wind.

"Josefina," she said, "I do love to hear you sing!" She

smiled. "Perhaps you'll sing a special song for all the village to hear as part of the Christmas celebration this year."

Josefina could feel her own smile sink right off her face. "Oh, no, Tía Dolores!" she said quickly, too surprised to be polite. She spoke again, this time with more respect. "I mean, I beg your pardon, but no, thank you."

"Why not?" asked Tía Dolores. "A lovely voice like yours is a gift from God. I am sure God means you to use it to delight others, especially if you do so to celebrate Him."

Josefina thought of how it would feel to have everyone looking at her, everyone listening to her singing all alone. She shivered. It was scarier than lightning. "I'm . . . sorry," she said, stumbling over the words. "I just *couldn't*."

Tía Dolores looked Josefina straight in the eye. "You mean you don't *want* to," she said. "But perhaps one day you will."

Josefina felt something jab her arm. It was a sprig of rabbit brush. Francisca was poking her with it.

Francisca raised one eyebrow and gave Josefina a look that said, *You see? Remember what I said about Tía Dolores poking and prodding us to be different than we are? Wasn't I right?*

The First Love

A few nights later, Josefina sat close to the fire in the family sala. The evening air had a sharpness that warned of the wintry cold to come. Josefina and Clara were spinning wool into yarn. Ana was putting her boys to bed. Francisca sat nearby sewing her fancy dress, which she still had not finished.

Tía Dolores was at her writing desk, bent close to her work. *Scritch, scratch, scritch, scratch.* Josefina loved the sound Tía Dolores's quill pen made as she wrote in the ledger she used to keep track of the weaving business. Paper and ink were precious, so Tía Dolores made her numbers small and filled every inch of every page. Papá sat nearby at the table, quietly watching her write.

Josefina looked around the family sala. *A piano, a writing desk, paper, pen, ink, and a ledger!* she thought. *Tía Dolores has brought so many new things to this room, Mamá wouldn't recognize it!* But Tía Dolores's things were not the only changes. Papá looked different, too. His face looked less tired, as if he were not so weighed down with sorrow as he had been, and sometimes he even whistled again, as he used to.

"There!" said Tía Dolores. She put her pen down with a pleased expression. "Would you do me the honor of looking at the figures?" she asked Papá.

"Sí," said Papá. Tía Dolores brought the ledger to the table, and she and Papá looked at it together.

"This shows how many sacks of wool we have," explained Tía Dolores as she pointed to a column of figures in the ledger. "And this shows how many blankets I think we can weave. And this shows how many sheep we'll get when we trade the blankets."

Papá nodded. "Excellent," he said. "The weaving business should do very well, God willing. I am grateful to you, Dolores." He patted the ledger. "It is fortunate that you can read and write."

"My aunt taught me when I lived with her in Mexico City," said Tía Dolores. She thought for a moment, and then she said, "And now, with your permission, I'll teach your daughters to read and write. Then they will be able to continue the weaving business after I leave."

Francisca gasped. Josefina knew that meant she was not happy at the thought of yet another new thing to do. Now they would have lessons in reading and writing on top of everything else!

Tía Dolores must have heard and understood the gasp, too, because she said, "The lessons won't add any time to the day. I have a little speller I brought with me from Mexico City. We'll use it when we sit by the fire at night. We will be putting our evenings to *very* good use."

Francisca spoke up boldly. "I don't see the need for learning to read and write," she said. "I have no time to read books, and no one ever sends letters that have anything to do with *me*."

Tía Dolores smiled. "Ah, but soon they will, Francisca!" she said. "Soon your papá will be receiving letters from young men who want to marry you."

Francisca sniffed. "Hmph!" she said. "I won't read them! And I'll reply to any marriage proposal by handing the young man the squash."

"That's true," stated Clara. "She's already done it!" In fact, a young man had already proposed to Francisca. She had indeed followed the old custom of giving him a squash to let him know she was not interested in marrying him.

"Letters proposing marriage can be very persuasive," said Tía Dolores. "Your papá won your mamá's heart with his letters!"

Francisca's dark eyes were flinty. "Mamá could not read," she said.

"No," said Tía Dolores. "But she always said that she loved the way your papá signed his name with such fancy flourishes."

Papá laughed. "I was young and foolish," he said. "It was the custom to make flourishes to show what an important person you were, and to make your signature different from anyone else's. I don't bother with flourishes anymore."

"Please, won't you show us how you used to do it, Papá?" asked Josefina.

Papá smiled but shook his head. "No, no. It's a waste of paper," he said.

"Not at all," said Tía Dolores. She handed him the pen and the green glass inkwell.

"Very well," said Papá agreeably. Josefina stood next to him and Clara peered over his shoulder. As they watched, Papá wrote his name in handsome, upright letters. Then, under his name, Papá made graceful swirls and curving spirals that looked like a long, lovely curl of ribbon.

"Oh, Papá, it's beautiful!" said Josefina. She turned to Tía Dolores. "Will we really learn to write like that?" she asked.

"Sí!" said Tía Dolores. "We'll begin tomorrow."

Josefina stared at Papá's beautiful writing. Then she looked up to smile at Francisca.

Surely Francisca would enjoy learning to do something as fancy and elegant-looking as this!

But Francisca was gone. She had slipped out quietly, without saying good night or waiting for Papá's blessing.

✳

Something woke Josefina in the middle of the night. It was a sound, just a small sound, but one that made Josefina sit up and tilt her head and listen hard. As her eyes adjusted to the darkness, Josefina saw that Francisca was not in her bed. Quietly, so as not to wake Clara, Josefina pulled on her moccasins, wrapped herself in her blanket, and crept outside.

Francisca was sitting in the courtyard. She was wrapped in her blanket, too. There was no moon, but the stars were so big and bright that Josefina could see Francisca's face. It was streaked with tears.

Josefina was surprised. She had not seen Francisca cry since Mamá died. "Francisca!" Josefina whispered as she came near. "What's the matter?"

"Go away," said Francisca fiercely.

Josefina knelt down next to her sister. "Are you ill?" she asked. "Shall I fetch Tía Dolores?"

"No!" said Francisca, with such force that Josefina was startled. "I've had quite enough of Tía Dolores!"

"What do you mean?" asked Josefina.

Francisca wiped the tears off her cheeks with an impatient hand. "Don't you see what's happening?" she asked. "Has Tía Dolores's praise for your sewing and weaving made you blind? Has she made you feel like such an important person that you don't care how she's changing everything? Nothing is the same as it was when Mamá was alive."

Suddenly the bitterness left Francisca's voice. It was replaced by sadness. "Every change makes Mamá seem farther and farther away," she said. "Every change makes me feel as if I'm losing Mamá again. And oh, Josefina! I miss Mamá so!"

"So do I," said Josefina passionately. Her heart ached with sympathy for Francisca. Now she saw why Francisca had complained about Tía Dolores. Josefina tried to make Francisca feel better. "I miss Mamá, too," she said. "But Tía Dolores is good and kind! She is only trying to help us."

"By changing us!" said Francisca. "Now she's going to make us learn to read and write. Mamá didn't read or write. Mamá didn't ask anyone to teach us to read or write. Reading and writing will be one more way Tía Dolores will pull us away from Mamá. It'll be just one more way she'll fill our heads and our hearts so that we'll have no room left for Mamá. We'll start to forget her. We've already started."

"Oh, Francisca!" said Josefina. "That's not true!" But a dark fear stole into Josefina's mind. Was Francisca right? It was true that Tía Dolores had changed their lives. Josefina herself had changed. Hadn't she braved the lightning? Hadn't she learned to weave? But did Tía Dolores's new ideas and new ways mean there was no room for the old ways? Was  Tía Dolores making them forget Mamá?

Francisca straightened her shoulders. "I am not going to do it," she said firmly. "I won't learn to read and write." She stood up and looked down at Josefina. "You'll have to make your own choice," she said. "Decide for yourself." Then she left.

Josefina stayed alone in the courtyard. She looked up at the huge, endless black sky and felt as if she were adrift in it. The stars seemed to be all around her—above her and below her and surrounding her on every side. Josefina felt lost. Francisca made it sound as if learning to read would be disloyal to Mamá. She made it seem as if Josefina had to choose between Mamá and Tía Dolores, between the old and the new.

What should I do, Mamá? Josefina asked. But she knew there would be no answer. The stars were as silent as stones.

✹

Usually Josefina skipped and sang all the way to the stream on laundry day. But today she walked joylessly, thinking about the conversation she'd had with Francisca the night before.

Tía Dolores was waiting for Josefina by the stream. "There you are, Josefina!" she said cheerfully. "You're as quiet as a little shadow this morning. And where are your sisters?"

"They're helping Carmen in the kitchen," Josefina answered.

"Good!" said Tía Dolores. "Then after we do the laundry, you will have your first reading lesson by yourself!"

Josefina tried to smile.

If Tía Dolores noticed that Josefina was not paying much attention to the clothes she was washing, she was too kind to say anything about it. They worked in an unusual silence. Tía Dolores spread a freshly washed white cloth on a bush to dry. There were already three other white cloths on the bush. "Look, Josefina!" said Tía Dolores with laughter in her voice. "They're four white doves perched on a rosemary bush!"

Josefina's face lit up for the first time that day. "Oh!" she said. "Mamá used to say that poem sometimes!" She tried to recite the whole poem. "'Behold four little white doves,

perched on a rosemary bush. They were . . . they were . . .'"
Josefina faltered. "I can't remember the rest," she said sadly.

Tía Dolores nodded. "Don't let it trouble you," she said.
She draped another cloth on the bush.

Josefina sighed so deeply and so unhappily that Tía
Dolores gave her a questioning look. "Oh, Tía Dolores,"
Josefina said, full of misery. "It *does* worry me. I can keep
things that remind me of Mamá in my memory box, but
I can't keep her words anywhere, and I'm beginning to for-
get them. It makes me afraid that I'm beginning to forget
Mamá herself."

Tía Dolores's eyes were gentle as she listened. When
Josefina stopped talking, Tía Dolores dried her hands on
her skirt and said, "Come with me, Josefina."

Josefina had to run to keep up with Tía Dolores's long
strides. Tía Dolores led Josefina back to the house and
into the family sala. Her writing desk was still there on its
stand. Without saying a word, Tía Dolores opened the lid
of the writing desk and pulled out a drawer. From a secret
compartment in the drawer she took a little book bound in
soft brown leather. She handed it to Josefina.

Very, very carefully, Josefina turned the pages of the
book. She couldn't read the words, but on many pages
there were little sketches. Josefina stopped when she came
to a drawing of four white birds perched on a bush.

Tía Dolores read the words on the page aloud:

> Behold four little white doves
> perched on a rosemary bush.
> They were saying to each other,
> "There's no love like the first love."

As she listened, Josefina remembered hearing Mamá's own dear voice, low and lilting and full of love, saying those very words.

"Your mamá didn't read or write," said Tía Dolores. "She learned this poem by hearing our papá read it aloud to us when we were little girls. When I was in Mexico City, I made this book. In it I wrote prayers, poems, songs, stories, even funny sayings your mamá and I both loved when we were girls. It helped me feel close to her, even though I was far away." She smiled at Josefina. "When you learn to read and write, you can look in this book anytime you like and read your mamá's words. In it you can write things you remember her saying. This book will be a place to keep her words safe, so that you'll never lose them."

Josefina smiled with tremendous relief and gladness. She felt as if she had received an answer from Mamá herself about what she should do. It was as if Mamá were

encouraging her to learn to read and write. Francisca was
wrong. Reading and writing wouldn't pull them away
from Mamá—it would help them remember her.

"Oh, please will you teach me to read this book?"
Josefina asked Tía Dolores.

"This book and any other you like!" said Tía Dolores.
"Reading is a way to hold on to the past, to travel to places
you've never been, and to learn about worlds beyond your
own time or experience. You'll find there are many grander

books than this one! Would you like to keep this little book with your memory box to be your very own?"

"No, gracias," said Josefina. She smiled a little smile. "That wouldn't be putting it to good use! I think you ought to keep it and read to all of us from it sometimes."

"Very well," said Tía Dolores.

"But may I borrow it for a moment?" Josefina asked. "I'll be careful."

"Sí, of course!" said Tía Dolores.

"Gracias!" said Josefina.

With a light heart and light feet, Josefina ran to find Francisca. She was sweeping in the kitchen.

"Look, Francisca!" said Josefina breathlessly. She opened Tía Dolores's little book to the drawing of the four doves. "The words on this page are Mamá's poem about the four doves," she said. "Do you remember it?"

Francisca thought. "Just the last line," she said. "I think it ends, 'There's no love like the first love.'"

"Sí!" said Josefina. "This whole book is filled with prayers and poems and sayings of Mamá's. Tía Dolores made it. Don't you see, Francisca? When we can read this book, it will be like hearing Mamá's voice. And when we can write, we can add things we remember her saying. This book will be a place to keep her words safe forever." Josefina put the book into Francisca's hands.

Francisca looked at the book and smiled. She didn't say anything, but her eyes were shining.

Josefina smiled back. "Come with me," she said. "Perhaps Tía Dolores will read more to us."

The two sisters hurried to the family sala. "Tía Dolores," said Josefina, "Francisca would like to hear you read something of Mamá's from your book. Would you read to us?"

"With pleasure," answered Tía Dolores. "But first, I would like to write your names in the book."

Francisca and Josefina watched eagerly while Tía Dolores dipped her pen in the ink. "This is your name, Francisca," she said.

Scritch, scratch, the pen moved across the page in the small book. "And now I'll write your name, Josefina."

"Be sure to add lots of flourishes," said Francisca, "to show what an important person she is!"

"I will!" said Tía Dolores. She wrote:

María Josefina Montoya

Christmas Is Coming

he wind was playing with Josefina. First it made her skirt billow out behind her and the ends of her rebozo fly up like wings. Then it swirled around and pushed against her back, hurrying her along like a helpful but impatient hand. Josefina smiled. She could see that the wind was playing with her sisters and Tía Dolores, too. They looked like birds with ruffled feathers as they were blown along the road on this blustery morning on their way to the village. Christmas was coming, and today everyone was gathering to clean the church so that it would be ready.

"Oh!" exclaimed Francisca, exasperated. The wind was blowing her hair so that it curled wildly around her face. She pulled her rebozo up over her head and tried to hold it in place with one hand as she struggled to carry a basket in her other hand.

Josefina slipped her arm under Francisca's basket. "I'll carry this," she said. She glanced at the bright red chiles in the basket. "Oh, good! You remembered the chiles for Señora Sánchez." She explained to Tía Dolores, "Mamá always gave Señora Sánchez some of our  chiles at this time of year. Señora Sánchez claimed she couldn't make her traditional stew without them."

Tía Dolores smiled. "I'm eager to taste Señora Sánchez's famous stew," she said. "I'm glad Christmas is coming."

Josefina could only manage a very small smile in return. She saw that Clara was frowning. Ana and Francisca didn't look very enthusiastic, either.

Tía Dolores looked at the sisters' faces. "What's the matter?" she asked.

Ana answered. "When Mamá was alive, Christmas was always happy," she said. "But last Christmas was the first one after Mamá died. All we could think of was how much we missed her."

Tía Dolores spoke quietly. "It must have been very hard."

Josefina slid her hand into Tía Dolores's. She knew that last Christmas must have been hard for her, too. Tía Dolores had been far away in Mexico City when Mamá, her sister, died. How sad and lonely she must have been!

"Last year, Christmas was very quiet," said Francisca. "There were no parties or dances, out of respect for Mamá. No one felt like celebrating anyway."

For a while the sisters and Tía Dolores walked without talking. Josefina listened to the stream as it splashed over rocks and around curves. The stream flowed steadily and cheerfully. Josefina wished she could be as carefree about the holiday that lay ahead.

She asked Tía Dolores about one thing that was worrying her. "Would it be wrong to be happy this Christmas?" she asked. "Would it be disrespectful to Mamá?"

"No, I don't think so," said Tía Dolores. "The time of mourning has passed. Christmas is a blessed time. I'm sure God means for us to be happy, and to celebrate the birth of His son, Jesús." She looked down at Josefina. "And I'm sure your mamá would want you to be happy. She'd want you to pray and sing and celebrate with your neighbors."

"Sí," Ana agreed. "Mamá would want us to follow all the Christmas traditions."

"I think so, too," said Francisca.

"Well," Clara said flatly. "We may follow the traditions, but they won't be the same without Mamá."

Somewhere inside Josefina a knot tightened. *Clara is right,* she thought. "Mamá loved Christmas traditions," Josefina said to Tía Dolores. "She even started a new one in our family. Every Christmas, she'd make a doll dress for—"

"Oh, Josefina!" exclaimed Ana, interrupting. "You're talking about Niña, aren't you? Niña should have been given to you last Christmas."

"But she never was," said Josefina.

Tía Dolores looked puzzled. "Who's Niña?" she asked.

Ana explained, "When I was eight, Mamá made a doll for me. She named the doll Niña. Every Christmas, Mamá made a new dress for Niña. Then, the year Francisca was eight, I gave Niña to her."

"Sí," said Francisca. "And the Christmas when Clara was eight, I gave Niña to *her*."

"Of course, last year Mamá was not here to make a dress for Niña," said Ana sadly. She turned to Clara. "But you could have given Niña to Josefina anyway, Clara. What happened?"

Josefina was curious to hear Clara's answer.

But Clara only shrugged and said, "I guess I forgot."

"Never mind, Clara," said Tía Dolores. "You can give the doll to Josefina this Christmas. I'll help you make a new dress for her. Where is Niña? I've never seen her."

"I haven't seen her in a long time, either," said Francisca.

"Neither have I," said Josefina, looking at Clara.

"Oh, she's around somewhere," said Clara. Her voice sounded unworried, but just for a second, a troubled look clouded her eyes. The look came and went so quickly, Josefina thought she must have imagined it.

Francisca, who was messy, liked to tease Clara, who was neat. "Heavens!" she said. "Do you mean to say that you've *lost* Niña?"

"She's not lost," said Clara crossly, "I'll find her!"

"Of course you will, Clara," said Tía Dolores.

Tía Dolores sounded so sure that Clara would find Niña. Josefina wished *she* could be as sure. How could Clara possibly have misplaced something as precious as Niña? Where could the doll be? At that moment, Josefina made up her mind. She was going to look for Niña herself, no matter what Clara said. After all, Niña was *supposed* to be hers.

Josefina's decision to look for Niña cheered her. She couldn't help feeling a little hopeful, just as she couldn't help feeling a little excited because she heard music floating up from the village urging, *Come along! Come along!* The music mixed in the air with the spicy scent of burning piñón wood rising up from chimneys into the cloudless blue sky above the village.

Josefina knew everyone in all of the twelve families who lived in the village. She knew their houses, too, which seemed to lean toward each other like old friends. The houses were made of earth-colored adobe. They were surrounded by fenced pens for the animals and vegetable gardens now sleeping under winter blankets of brown dirt. The

houses faced the clean-swept *plaza* at the center of the
village. The biggest and most important building in the
village was the church, with its great bell hung high above
the front doors.

Today, the doors of the church were wide open. People
scurried in and out carrying brooms and brushes, tools,
and scrubbing rags. They hauled big, sloshing tubs of water
up from the stream.

"Buenos días! It's good to see you! How are you today?"
everyone called when they saw Tía Dolores and the sisters.

"Buenos días! We're very well, thank you," they called
back over music and the noise of dogs barking and ham-
mers pounding. People were talking, and every once in
a while Josefina would hear swoops of laughter from the
little children as they chased one another.

Clara, Francisca, and Ana went inside the church
to start working. But Tía Dolores and Josefina lingered
outside next to the musicians, who began to play a slow,
sweet song.

"I haven't heard this lullaby since I was a child," said
Tía Dolores. "Please, Josefina, will you sing it for me?"

Softly, Josefina sang:

> *Sleep, my beautiful baby,*
> *Sleep, my grain of gold.*

The night is very cold,
The night is . . .

Josefina's throat tightened, and she couldn't finish
the song. She turned her head away so that Tía Dolores
wouldn't see that her eyes had filled with tears.

But Tía Dolores had seen them already. She used the
soft edge of her sleeve to dry Josefina's cheek.

"Mamá used to sing that lullaby to me when I was
little," said Josefina. "Papá played it on his violin. And
we always sang it together at church on Christmas Eve to
baby Jesús. Everyone sings the end. The first part is sung
alone by the girl who is María in *Las Posadas*."

"You know," said Tía Dolores, "you're old enough to be
María."

"Oh, I couldn't!" said Josefina. Her heart pounded
faster at the very thought. Las Posadas was one of the
most important and holy Christmas traditions. For nine
nights in a row, everyone in the village acted out the
story of the first Christmas Eve, when María and José
were searching for shelter before baby Jesús was born.
A girl took the role of María, riding a burro just as Jesús's
mother did, and a man took the role of José. María and
José and their followers went from house to house asking for shelter. Again and again they were turned away,

until finally they were welcomed into the last house. On Christmas Eve, the last night of Las Posadas, everyone was welcomed into the church instead of a house, and then Midnight Mass began.

"Sometimes," said Tía Dolores thoughtfully, "a girl wants to be María because she wants to pray for something special. I wonder what your prayer would be, Josefina, if you were María?"

Josefina didn't have to wonder. She knew what her prayer would be. "I'd pray that this will be a happy Christmas," said Josefina, "for us and for Mamá in heaven."

Tía Dolores smiled. "That's a good prayer," she said. "Are you sure you don't want to be María?"

Josefina listened to the last notes of the lullaby. Part of her wanted to be María, but part of her knew she couldn't do it. "Last year, I could hardly sing the songs in Las Posadas," she said. "They made me so sad, because they reminded me that Mamá was gone. I'm afraid it'll be the same this year." She shook her head. "I couldn't possibly be María."

"I understand," said Tía Dolores. "It's still too soon for you." She tucked a strand of Josefina's hair behind her ear. "Let's go in now." Josefina nodded, and they walked into the church together.

The church was usually a quiet, solemn place, and dim because the windows were very small and set deep in the

thick walls. But today it was busy
and noisy. Light poured in from the
open doors and peeked through
gaps in the roof where it had been
damaged in the big storm.

Everywhere Josefina looked, she saw friends and neighbors, as well as workers from Papá's rancho who'd put aside
their usual chores to come and clean the church. Señora
Sánchez, Señora López, and several other women chatted
together as they swept. Josefina saw Papá's sister, Tía
Magdalena, with a group of women who were polishing
candlesticks. Ana, Francisca, and Clara were in a group of
girls who were dusting. Boys, who were supposed to be
scattering water over the floor to settle the dust, were splash-
ing each other. Most of the men of the village stood together,
their arms crossed over their chests, looking up at the roof
and discussing the damage caused by the storm in the fall.

Josefina saw Papá standing with the men. Then Papá
and Señor García came over. Señor García was the *mayordomo*. It was his job to assign tasks, because he and his
wife took care of the church. Señor García was an old
man, thin and stooped, with very white hair. He had a
husky voice and stately manners. Everyone respected him
for his knowledge and liked him for his kindness.

"God bless you for coming!" said Señor García. "The

roof caused terrible damage when it fell in. We have a lot to do before the priest, Padre Simón, comes on Christmas Eve. May I ask your family to wash and iron the altar cloth that your dear wife gave to the church?"

"Sí," said Papá quietly.

"And Josefina," said Señor García, "I was wondering if you would like to be María in Las Posadas this Christmas, perhaps to offer a special prayer for your mamá?"

Josefina froze. Papá looked at her, waiting to hear her answer.

Tía Dolores put her arm around Josefina's shoulders. "It's very kind of you to ask, Señor García," she said. "But I think not this year."

"Ah, I see, I see," said Señor García gently. "Perhaps next year . . . Well, well, Margarita Sánchez can be María this Christmas."

Josefina didn't say anything. She leaned against Tía Dolores, grateful for her understanding. Then she went to find Señora Sánchez to give her the basket of chiles.

The morning flew by so fast that Josefina was surprised when it was time say her good-byes. It had been nice to be part of the friendly group all scrubbing and sweeping and dusting together. Because of their work, the church shone. But now Josefina headed home with eager steps. She was determined to begin looking for Niña that very afternoon.

Where Is Niña?

CHAPTER 10

The last time Josefina had seen her, Niña was wearing a pale blue skirt. Her arms and legs were flat because some of her stuffing had fallen out, and her black yarn hair was tangled. Josefina clearly remembered Niña's lively black eyes and smiling pink mouth, and she was pretty sure she remembered a green sash tied around Niña's waist. *I'll just keep my eyes sharp for any bit of green or black or pale blue,* Josefina thought. *Niña has to be somewhere.*

Josefina searched every inch of the rancho: her sleeping sala, the grand sala, the kitchen, every nook and cranny of the storerooms, the stables, the chicken coops, and even in desperation, the goats' pen. Niña was nowhere to be found. Josefina tried hard not to be discouraged. *I'll search again tomorrow,* she decided.

That evening, Papá carried a battered trunk into the kitchen and set it down near the fire. "Mamá's altar cloth is in this trunk," Josefina said to Tía Dolores. "Wait till you see it! The birds that Mamá embroidered on it look so real that you expect them to sing!"

Tía Dolores smiled. She knelt next to the trunk. Papá

and all the sisters crowded around, peering over her shoulders as she opened the lid. Tía Dolores lifted the altar cloth out of the trunk and  they all looked at it. For a moment, no one said anything. Then Papá pulled his breath in sharply, as if something had hurt him. Without a word, he turned and left the room.

Josefina was confused. What was this torn, bedraggled cloth in Tía Dolores's hands? This cloth looked like a rag. It was chewed by mice. It smelled of mildew. It was water-stained and dirty. It couldn't be Mamá's beautiful embroidered altar cloth. But it was.

"Oh, no," said Ana, sounding miserable. "Water from the flood must have rotted the leather of the trunk so that mice and dampness got in. Just look at the damage."

"It's *ruined*!" Clara cried out. "It's ruined, just like Christmas!" She rushed from the room.

The door slammed behind her, and the whole room and everyone in it was shaken. It wasn't like Clara to act like that. Her words echoed in Josefina's head: *It's ruined, just like Christmas* ... The knot inside Josefina tightened again. Just when Josefina had begun to hope that this Christmas might be happy, *this* had to happen. The beautiful altar cloth Mamá had made so lovingly was destroyed. It hurt

◄ **93** ►

Josefina to look at it on Tía Dolores's lap.

Ana sighed. "I'm glad Mamá is not here to see this," she said. "It would break her heart."

Tía Dolores examined the cloth carefully, running her hands over it. Then she said, "I think we can repair this."

Ana, Francisca, and Josefina looked at each other. "But how?" asked Francisca.

"First, we'll wash it," said Tía Dolores. "Then we'll iron it. We'll replace the embroidery the mice chewed away with new embroidery."

Francisca looked doubtful. "We'll need Clara for that," she said. "Mamá taught us all *colcha* embroidery, but Clara's the best at it. She's the only one who's even close to doing colcha as well as Mamá."

"Very well," said Tía Dolores. "Josefina, please go to Clara and ask her to come back so that I may speak to her."

Josefina nodded. Quickly, she crossed the courtyard to the room she shared with Francisca and Clara. The door was partly open, and through it Josefina heard the sound of Clara crying. Josefina stood still, not sure what to do. As she hesitated, she looked into the room. It was dark, but Josefina saw Clara open the clothes trunk and take out an old skirt that was neatly folded into a thick bundle. Clara unfolded the skirt. Josefina saw a bit of something pale blue, a flash of green, *and there was Niña!*

Josefina gasped in surprise and
bewilderment. Clara had Niña! The
doll had been hidden in Clara's trunk
all this time! Josefina took one step into
the room, then stopped short when she saw Clara bury her
face in Niña and sob. Clara cried as if her heart was broken, and she held on to Niña as if the doll were her only
comfort in the world. Josefina turned away quietly so that
Clara wouldn't hear her.

When Josefina got back to the kitchen, Ana and
Francisca were gone. Tía Dolores was alone, still holding
the altar cloth.

"Is Clara coming?" asked Tía Dolores.

"No," said Josefina. Suddenly, she burst out, "Clara has
Niña! I saw her! The door was open and when I looked in,
I saw Clara holding the doll!" Josefina spoke as if she could
hardly believe what she had seen. "Clara has known where
Niña is all along. She's been keeping her for herself!"

Tía Dolores put the altar cloth down and took Josefina's
hands in her own. "I'm not sure I understand it," she said
slowly. "But your mamá made Niña, and she made a new
dress for her every Christmas. So Niña is a way for Clara to
feel close to your mamá. She's a comfort. Clara needs her."

"But why did she pretend she didn't know where Niña
was?" asked Josefina indignantly. "That wasn't *true*."

"Do you remember when you told me how you're not ready to be María in Las Posadas?" Tía Dolores asked.

Josefina nodded.

"Well, Clara is not ready to give you Niña. That's why she's hiding her," said Tía Dolores. She looked at Josefina's long face and tried to cheer her. "At least we know that Niña isn't lost. She's safe. That's good, isn't it?"

"I guess so," Josefina admitted grudgingly. "But when will Clara give her to me? Will Niña ever be mine?"

Tía Dolores sighed. "I don't know," she said. "No one knows, probably not even Clara. It may take a long time." She put Josefina's hands aside and picked up the altar cloth again. "Just as it will take time to repair this altar cloth. But we'll do it. The sooner we begin, the better." Tía Dolores tried to tease a smile out of Josefina. "What do I always say?" she asked.

Josefina had to smile just a little bit, in spite of Clara, in spite of Niña, and in spite of herself. "You always say, 'The saints cry over lost time.'"

"Precisely!" said Tía Dolores briskly. "We'll start tomorrow!"

The Silver Thimble

A nd they did start repairing the altar cloth the very next day—everyone except Clara. Josefina helped Tía Dolores wash the altar cloth in warm, soapy water and rinse it in clear, cool water. Gently, Tía Dolores wrung out the cloth. Then she and Josefina spread it to dry in a sunny corner of the back courtyard. When the cloth was dry, Ana ironed it smooth, being careful not to scorch it with the hot irons heated by the fire. Francisca helped Josefina mend some of the holes the mice had chewed, and Tía Dolores cut off the end where the holes were too big to mend. She attached a new piece of material in its place.

At last the time came to begin the colcha embroidery. Tía Dolores and the four sisters gathered in front of the fire as they did every evening. Tía Dolores spread out the altar cloth. "What shall we embroider?" she asked, looking at the sisters.

Josefina looked at the altar cloth. Firelight brightened the colors of the designs that Mamá had stitched. Josefina had an idea. "Mamá made the altar cloth," she said. "I think we should embroider things on it that she loved."

"Mamá loved swallows," Francisca said. "I'll embroider swallows and other birds on the altar cloth."

"I'll stitch sprigs of lavender," said Ana. "Mamá loved its scent."

"And I'll embroider leaves and flowers," said Josefina. "Because Mamá loved them."

"And what will you embroider, Clara?" Tía Dolores asked.

Clara was only halfway in the firelight. She looked at the altar cloth with critical eyes. "It doesn't matter," she said. "We can't make that cloth look right again without Mamá anyway."

"We can," said Tía Dolores firmly. "It'll take time, but we can repair it. And if we all work together, I think we'll even enjoy doing it."

Clara drew back out of the light, but Josefina saw her face. It looked as sad as it did in the moment Josefina had seen Clara holding Niña and crying. Suddenly, Josefina felt sorry for Clara.

"Doing the colcha embroidery makes me miss Mamá, too, Clara," Josefina said. "It makes her seem very far away, doesn't it?"

Clara didn't answer.

"Perhaps this will help," said Tía Dolores. She reached in

her pocket and took out a silver thimble. "Your mamá gave this to me a long time ago when we were girls. She was trying to teach me how to do colcha. I didn't like it because I kept pricking myself with the needle and it hurt. She gave me the thimble to protect my finger. Now all of you may use it to protect *your* fingers."

Clara leaned forward on her stool. "If Mamá gave something like that to me, I'd keep it forever," she said. "I wouldn't dream of giving it away!"

Just like Niña, thought Josefina with a heavy heart.

"But it makes me happy to share the thimble," said Tía Dolores. "When we use it, we'll think of your mamá with every stitch we make. Perhaps it will make her seem closer, not farther away."

"Oh, please, may I use it?" Josefina asked.

Tía Dolores handed the silver thimble to Josefina, and she put it on her finger. It looked shiny in the light of the fire. As she began stitching, Josefina used the thimble to help push the needle through the cloth. She knew Clara was watching her. When Josefina started to tie a knot at the end of the wool she was using, Clara moved next to her.

"Don't," said Clara. "Have you forgotten? Mamá said never to knot the wool. Use your second stitch to hold your first stitch in place. Here, let me show you. I'll stitch the stem of that flower for you."

Clara spread the cloth over her knees and took the needle from Josefina. She began to stitch. Francisca nudged Ana, and Ana raised her eyebrows at Josefina as if to say, *This is a surprise!*

Josefina took the thimble off her finger. "Use this," she said.

Clara stopped for a moment and looked at the thimble. Then, slowly, she took it from Josefina and slipped it on her own finger. "Gracias," she said, but so quietly only Josefina could hear her.

Josefina gave herself the job of untangling knots in the wool Tía Dolores was using. When she looked up a little while later, Josefina saw that Clara had finished stitching the stem and was embroidering a yellow blossom on the end of it. Josefina saw that Clara's stitches were smooth and sure and secure.

She also saw that Clara hadn't taken the silver thimble off her finger.

✿

The four sisters and Tía Dolores worked on the cloth almost every evening, and it was a time Josefina looked forward to. They took turns wearing the silver thimble. Francisca made a game out of it. She said that whoever wore the thimble had to share a memory about Mamá. Sometimes the memories would make Josefina sad. But sometimes they made her laugh because they reminded her of happy times. Just as the thimble protected Josefina and her sisters from the pain of being pricked by the needle, it seemed also to protect them from the pain that memories of Mamá used to bring.

Repairing the altar cloth was slow work. But as the days went by, stitch by stitch the cloth became beautiful again. And as the days went by, bit by bit Josefina began to feel better about all the things this Christmas might bring—even though she was now quite sure Niña was not going to be one of them.

La Noche Buena

CHAPTER 12

E very day was colder than the one before, and
Christmas Eve was bone-chilling. The sky was
as dark as stone from dawn till dusk, and sleet fell without
stopping. Josefina's hands were stiff as she and Clara put
the final stitches in the altar cloth late that afternoon.

At last the cloth was finished. Tía Dolores held one
end and Ana held the other so that they could fold it carefully. One of the flowers Clara had embroidered ended up
on top. Tía Dolores stroked the flower gently. "Clara," she
said. "You have your mamá's gift for embroidery. Truly
you do."

"I can't tell Clara's flowers from those Mamá made,"
agreed Ana.

A quick, pleased smile lit Clara's face. She took the
silver thimble off her finger and held it out to Tía Dolores.
"Thank you for sharing this with us," she said.

Tía Dolores didn't take the thimble. Instead she said,
"Keep it. Go put it safely away in your sala. And Josefina,
you'd better go, too. It's time for you girls to change your
clothes." She smiled. "It's Christmas Eve!"

Josefina and Clara hurried across the courtyard to their room. Francisca, who shared the room with them, had finished dressing. She'd left a small candle burning to give Clara and Josefina light to dress by. But as they came in, it seemed to Josefina that the room was illuminated by more than one small candle. Josefina smiled when she saw why.

Someone had laid out Josefina's best black lace *mantilla*, her comb, and her new dress on top of the trunk. The pretty yellow dress brightened the whole room. Josefina walked toward it, then stopped, stared, and gasped in surprise. For there, sitting on top of her yellow dress, was Niña!

mantilla

Josefina lifted Niña up. She saw that Niña's face looked just as she remembered it. The eyes Mamá had sewn out of black thread still looked lively, and the mouth Mamá had sewn out of pink thread still smiled sweetly. Niña's yarn hair was smooth and untangled. Her arms and legs were plump with new stuffing. Best of all, Niña had a new yellow dress that exactly matched Josefina's. It had a long skirt and long sleeves gathered in puffs up near the shoulders. Niña even had a tiny new mantilla like Josefina's. Josefina hugged Niña and kissed her soft cheeks.

"She's yours," said Clara.

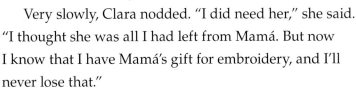

"Oh, Clara!" Josefina whispered. "Gracias!" She hugged Niña closer. "I thought she never would be. I...I knew that you had her, and I—"

"Why didn't you say anything?" Clara asked.

"Well," said Josefina, "Tía Dolores told me that you needed her."

Very slowly, Clara nodded. "I did need her," she said. "I thought she was all I had left from Mamá. But now I know that I have Mamá's gift for embroidery, and I'll never lose that."

Josefina touched the smooth ribbon around the high waist of Niña's dress. "Did you make this dress for Niña?" Josefina asked.

"Sí," said Clara. "I wanted to carry on the tradition that Mamá started."

Josefina smiled broadly at Clara. "Niña's dress is beautiful," she said. "I think maybe you have Mamá's gift for making doll dresses, too!"

Clara smiled back. Then she looked lovingly at Niña. "I went to Niña for comfort because I thought I had nowhere else to go," she said. "But now I know that there's comfort all around me if I need it."

"Sí," said Josefina. "I'm finding that out also." She opened Clara's fist, and the silver thimble shone in the candlelight. "We'll share the thimble," Josefina said to Clara. "And we'll share Niña, too. She'll sleep between us from now on."

Christmas Eve was called *la Noche buena*—the good night. And this Christmas Eve felt like a very good night to Josefina. Niña was hers to love and care for at last. The weather was still sleety and cold, so Josefina wore a rebozo crisscrossed over her chest under the outer blanket she wore for warmth. She tucked Niña inside her rebozo and held her tight as she and her family walked to the village.

A big bonfire glowed gold in the darkness in front of the church. Josefina was glad to see it. She was glad to go inside the church, too, where it was dry. Sleet had beaded her blanket as if it were covered with thousands of tiny pearls. Josefina took the blanket off and shook it just inside the door of the church. She checked to be sure that Niña was held safe in her rebozo, then hurried to catch up with Papá and Tía Dolores and her sisters. They were near the altar with Señor García and other friends and neighbors who had come to decorate the church.

Tía Dolores gave the altar cloth to Señor García.

"Gracias!" said Señor García to Tía Dolores and the

sisters. "I am told that all of you had to work hard to repair this. God bless you!"

"Everyone is grateful," added Señora Sánchez. "Now our altar will be as beautiful as it has been in years past. But pardon me, Señor García," she added breathlessly. "I have bad news. My daughter Margarita is too ill to be María tonight. She can't stir from her bed."

"Poor Margarita!" said Señor García.

Everyone gathered around Señora Sánchez and Señor García, murmuring, "Oh, the poor child. Bless her soul!"

Josefina's heart beat fast. She asked herself a question, and thought hard about the answer. Slipping one hand inside her rebozo so that it was touching Niña, Josefina used the other hand to tug gently on Señor García's sleeve.

Señor García turned to her. Josefina's voice was small but steady as she looked up at him and said, "Please, Señor García, may I be María?" Everyone looked at Josefina as she went on, "I'd like to pray that this will be a happy Christmas for us and for my mamá in heaven."

Señor García's thin old face was solemn. Slowly, he nodded. "Sí, my child," he said to Josefina. "You may be María."

Josefina turned to Papá. "Will you be José?" she asked.

"I will," said Papá gravely. He didn't smile, but he looked at Josefina with pride and love. Tía Dolores did, too.

✤

When it was time for Las Posadas, Josefina handed Niña to Clara for safekeeping. "Please hold her for me," Josefina said. "Keep her warm."

Clara took the doll. "I will," she promised.

They all went outside. The wind was blowing hard, driving the sleet so that it stung Josefina's face. Papá lifted Josefina up onto the burro's back. She knew Señor Sánchez's burro was gentle. But still, she felt very high off the ground. Josefina was glad Papá would be walking at her side leading the burro. She took the reins and held on tight as Papá draped another blanket over her. "This will keep you warm," he said.

As the villagers gathered to begin the procession, many people stopped to speak to Papá and Josefina. "May God grant you a good and long life," they said.

Josefina tried to sit up as straight as she could on the burro's back. Then, with a *clop clop* of the burro's hooves on the frozen ground, they moved to the first house.

Papá knocked on the door, and they all sang:

In heaven's name, we ask for shelter.

And the people inside sang back:

This is not an inn! Be on your way!

Josefina's voice was unsteady at first. She felt nervous and stiff. But the lovely music and words soon made her forget all about herself and her shyness. Soon Josefina was singing the Las Posadas songs in a voice that was full of all the hope and happiness of Christmas.

Papá led the burro from house to house. At each house, he and Josefina and everyone with them sang, asking for shelter. And at each house, the people inside sang back, telling them to go away. Then everyone inside the house came out to join the group behind Papá. After the last house, Papá turned back to the church. By that time, everyone in the whole village and all the workers from the rancho were in the crowd. Josefina felt as if everyone she knew and loved in the world were there behind her.

When they got to the church, Papá knocked on the doors. *Boom! Boom! Boom!* The sound echoed inside. Then everyone sang:

> *María, Queen of Heaven, begs for shelter*
> *For just one night, kind sir!*

Padre Simón opened one of the church doors just a bit. He looked out and sang:

> *Come in, weary travelers. You are welcome!*

Then Padre Simón flung both doors open wide. Golden candlelight flooded out. The church bell rang. And everyone sang:

> *God bless you for your kindness,*
> *And may heaven fill you with peace and joy!*

Papá lifted Josefina down off the burro. She was glad

for his strong arms, because her legs felt wobbly and numb from the cold.

"Josefina," she heard someone whisper. It was Clara, who handed Niña to her. Josefina tucked Niña safe inside her rebozo again.

Then Tía Dolores took Josefina by one hand and Papá took the other, and they walked into the church behind Padre Simón. Ana, Francisca, Clara, and everyone else followed.

Josefina could hardly breathe. The church was so beautiful, she felt as if she were walking into a dream. All the candles were lit. Their brightness made the candlesticks shine and the polished wood glow. The candles cast a warm light on the Nativity scene in its nest of pine branches.

But to Josefina, the most beautiful thing by far was Mamá's altar cloth. Perhaps it was because she knew and

 loved every stitch of it after working on it for so long with Tía Dolores and her sisters. In the wavering candlelight, the soft, flowing leaves and flowers seemed to be floating in a gentle breeze, and the colors were rich and true. Josefina looked at the newly embroidered flowers with pride. *Mamá would be pleased*, she thought.

By now the church was full of people, and Padre

Simón began the Mass. When it was time for her to sing
the beginning of the lullaby, Josefina stood up, closed her
eyes, and sang:

> *Sleep, my beautiful baby,*
> *Sleep, my grain of gold.*

Her voice was the only sound in the church, like a bird
singing all alone on a mountaintop. Then Josefina opened
her eyes, and everyone sang with her:

> *The night is very cold,*
> *The night is very cold.*

Josefina listened to all the voices soaring up around
her, and she felt as safe and as loved as she used to feel
when Mamá sang the lullaby to her.

Josefina hugged Niña close, sure that her
prayer for a happy Christmas had
been answered.

Glossary of Spanish Words

Abuelito *(ah-bweh-LEE-toh)*—Grandpa

adiós *(ah-dee-OHS)*—good-bye

adobe *(ah-DOH-beh)*—a building material made of earth mixed with straw and water

americano *(ah-meh-ree-KAH-no)*—a man from the United States

arroyo *(ah-RO-yo)*—a gully or dry riverbed with steep sides

buenos días *(BWEH-nohs DEE-ahs)*—good morning

Camino Real *(kah-MEE-no rey-AHL)*—the trail that ran from Mexico City to New Mexico. Its name means "Royal Road."

colcha *(KOHL-chah)*—a kind of embroidery with long, flat stitches

fandango *(fahn-DAHNG-go)*—a big party that includes a lively dance

gracias *(GRAH-see-ahs)*—thank you

gran sala *(grahn SAH-lah)*—the biggest room in the house, used for special events and formal occasions

la Noche buena *(lah NO-cheh BWEH-nah)*—Christmas Eve

Las Posadas *(lahs po-SAH-dahs)*—a drama that tells the story of the first Christmas Eve. It means "The Inns."

mantilla *(mahn-TEE-yah)*—a lacy scarf that girls and women wear over their head and shoulders

mayordomo *(mah-yor-DOH-mo)*—a man who is elected to take charge of town or church affairs

Padre *(PAH-dreh)*—the title for a priest. It means "Father."

patrón *(pah-TROHN)*—a man who has earned respect because he owns land and manages it well, and is a good leader

piñón *(pee-NYOHN)*—a kind of short, scrubby pine that produces delicious nuts

plaza *(PLAH-sah)*—an open square in a village or town

pueblo *(PWEH-blo)*—a village of Pueblo Indians

rancho *(RAHN-cho)*—a farm or ranch where crops are grown and animals are raised

rebozo *(reh-BO-so)*—a long shawl worn by girls and women

sala *(SAH-lah)*—a room in a house

sí *(SEE)*—yes

siesta *(see-ES-tah)*—a rest or nap taken in the afternoon

tortilla *(tor-TEE-yah)*—a kind of flat, round bread made of corn or wheat

Inside
Josefina's World

Today, New Mexico is one of the 50 states in the United States. But in 1824, when Josefina was a girl, New Mexico was part of the country of Mexico. For hundreds of years before that, all of Mexico—including New Mexico—belonged to Spain.

Spanish settlers first came to New Mexico more than 400 years ago, in 1598—even before the Pilgrims landed in Plymouth, Massachusetts. They brought their language and customs with them. They spoke Spanish, kept their Catholic faith, and enjoyed music and dances from Spain. They built homes in the mountains and river valleys. Many New Mexicans today are related to these early settlers.

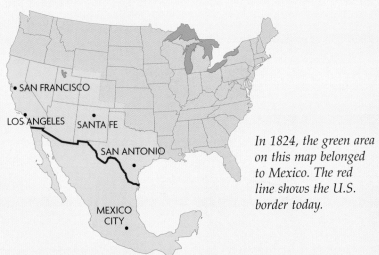

In 1824, the green area on this map belonged to Mexico. The red line shows the U.S. border today.

Most settlers lived on ranchos or in small villages. Villages were built around a central *plaza* with the church at the head. There were no shops, so families grew their own food and made their own clothes. It was hard to farm on the dry, mountainous land. Drought was a constant worry, and so were sudden floods caused by heavy rainstorms. Everyone worked hard. Women and girls gardened, cooked, and tended the home, while men and boys worked in the fields and herded the animals.

The Camino Real was a rugged trail used by traders, settlers, soldiers, and missionaries.

At the time Josefina's story opens, there was no trade between New Mexico and the United States, but there was trade with other parts of Mexico. The Camino Real, or Royal Road, connected Santa Fe, the capital, with Mexican towns and cities hundreds of miles south. For more than 200 years, the Camino Real was New Mexico's only link to the rest of the world. A caravan like Abuelito's took four or five months to travel from Santa Fe to Mexico City, where New Mexican products like wool blankets and hides could be traded for goods from around the world.

Trading caravans brought luxuries like silk, lace, and jewelry—such as this hair comb and necklace—as well as tools, books, and furniture to New Mexico.

This girl practices her sewing in the courtyard of her home.

Books were rare and treasured possessions for families who had them. Few New Mexican villages had schools, so most children were taught the same way Josefina was, by a family member at home. Girls learned the skills they needed to run a home of their own. Like Josefina, they were taught to sew, knit, spin, weave, cook, garden, and preserve food for the winter. Boys learned to plant and harvest crops, tend animals, and repair buildings and tools.

Girls and women spun yarn and wove blankets from the wool of their own sheep.

Music, dancing, and warm hospitality were all part of Christmas celebrations in Josefina's time, as they are today.

At Christmastime, people celebrated their Catholic faith and enjoyed evenings filled with friends and family. Women and girls cooked holiday treats and decorated their homes and church. Religious plays were an important part of Christmas, too, just as they had been for hundreds of years in Spain. Each village acted out Las Posadas or "The Inns," the story of Jesus's parents searching for lodging in Bethlehem. The people playing María and José (Mary and Joseph) went from house to house, asking for a place to stay. Villagers followed them, holding candles and singing hymns. At every house they were turned away until they came to the last house or the church, and the whole village was invited inside for music, dancing, and treats. Often the people who played María and José were praying for something special, just as Josefina was when she played María.

Today, New Mexican children still act out Las Posadas at Christmas, and they still love the lively music and spicy food that make life in New Mexico as magical today as it was in Josefina's time.

Second
Chances

Papá lifted the front corner of his *sarape*. Cradled in his arm was a tiny goat.

"Oh!" gasped Josefina. She reached out and touched the goat's silky little ear. The goat turned its head and nuzzled the palm of Josefina's hand. Suddenly, Josefina knew what she must do. "Please, Papá," she asked. "May I take care of Florecita's baby?"

Papá's face was full of concern. "The baby is very weak, Josefina," he said. "It isn't easy to care for an animal this needy. And you must realize that there's a good chance the baby won't live, even if you do care for her."

Josefina understood. Papá was afraid her heart would be broken. For a moment, Josefina was afraid, too. But then she looked at the little goat and all her doubts fell away.

Carefully, Papa put the baby goat into Josefina's arms. She held the soft warm body nestled close to her chest and rubbed her cheek against the goat's fur. The baby goat gave one small bleat, closed her eyes, and went to sleep as if Josefina's arms were the safest place in the world.

"Take her back to the house," said Papá, "and keep her next to the fire. I'll bring some milk. You'll have to teach her to drink. She's yours to care for now."

a Nez Perce girl who
loves daring adventures
on horseback

a Hispanic girl
growing up on a rancho
in New Mexico

who is determined
to be free in the midst
of the Civil War

a Jewish girl with
a secret ambition to
be an actress

who faces the
Great Depression with
determination and grit

who joins the
war effort when Hawaii
is attacked

whose big ideas get
her into trouble—but
also save the day

who finds the
strength to lift
for those wh

the
on the
all team